P9-CBT-396

J. T. EDSON'S
FLOATING OUTFIT

The toughest bunch of Rebels that ever lost a war, they fought for the South, and then for Texas, as the legendary Floating Outfit of "Ole Devil" Hardin's O.D. Connected ranch.

MARK COUNTER was the best dressed man in the West: always dressed fit-to-kill. BELLE BOYD was as deadly as she was beautiful, with a "Manhattan" model Colt tucked under her long skirts. THE YSABEL KID was Comanche fast and Texas tough. And the most famous of them all was DUSTY FOG, the ex-cavalryman known as the Rio Hondo Gun Wizard.

J. T. Edson has captured all the excitement and adventure of the raw frontier in this magnificent Western Series. Turn the page for a complete list of Floating Outfit titles.

J.T. Edson

A HORSE CALLED MOGOLLON

CHARTER BOOKS, NEW YORK

This Charter book contains the complete
text of the original edition.
It has been completely reset in a typeface
designed for easy reading and was printed
from new film.

A HORSE CALLED MOGOLLON

A Charter Book/published by arrangement with
Transworld Publishers, Ltd.

PRINTING HISTORY
Corgi edition published 1971
Berkley edition / May 1980
Charter edition / April 1988

All rights reserved.
Copyright © 1970 by J.T. Edson.
This book may not be reproduced in whole or in part,
by mimeograph or any other means, without permission.
For information address: Transworld Publishers, Ltd.,
c/o Writers House, Inc.,
21 West 26th St., New York, N.Y. 10010.

ISBN: 1-55773-018-0

Charter Books are published by The Berkley Publishing Group,
200 Madison Avenue, New York, NY 10016.
The name "Charter" and the "C" logo are
trademarks belonging to Charter Communications, Inc.

PRINTED IN THE UNITED STATES OF AMERICA

10   9   8   7   6   5   4   3   2   1

*For Pat Bacon. Keep selling my books,
Pat, I'm much too idle to go to work.*

CHAPTER ONE

"Hold it!" Jeanie Schell whispered urgently as her dainty dun gelding tossed its head back, snuffled the breeze and cocked its ears toward the top of the slope up which her party was riding. "There's hosses over the rim."

Immediately her two companions reined their mounts to a stop. Dusty Fog and Colin Farquharson had known the girl for long enough to be satisfied that she could read her gelding's reactions correctly.

Small, petite, her reddish-brown hair a short, curly halo about an attractively tanned, pretty face, Jeanie had worked with horses almost all her life and knew their moods. Not yet twenty, she had a well-formed body fast maturing to womanhood. A low-crowned, wide-brimmed grey Stetson perched on the back of her head. She wore a dark green shirt tucked into Levi's pants, the turned-back cuffs of which hung outside her high-heeled riding boots.

Like the girl, Dusty Fog had been born and raised in Texas, although they came from different backgrounds. His clan owned most of the land in Rio Hondo County. Jeanie's late father had been a mustanger, a catcher and breaker of wild horses, and her home wherever the family's wagon came to a halt.

Barely six inches taller than Jeanie's five-foot height, Dusty had a width to his shoulders that, taken with his slender waist, hinted at an exceptional muscular development. Despite their being expensive and well-tailored, he made his clothes look like somebody's hand-me-downs in a way which took most of the emphasis from his physique and made him appear almost insignificant. Not even the

1

excellent design and workmanship of his gunbelt, with twin bone-handled 1860 Army Colts in the cross-draw holsters, tended to render him more impressive at first glance.

If an observer chanced to examine him closer, certain facts grew into focus. There was much more to the short, dusty-blond cowhand than appeared on the surface. His magnificent seventeen hand paint stallion gave the first clue. Only a man of considerable equestrian ability could hope to remain on its back and control it and he sat the low-horned, double-girthed range saddle with an almost effortless ease. Tilted at the traditional "jack-deuce" angle over his right eye, his black Texas-style Stetson threw a shadow across a handsome face with strength, intelligence and power in its lines.

Maybe Dusty Fog presented a first impression of being a small nonentity, but few people in Texas regarded him in that light. During and since the recently ended War between the States, he had achieved an almost legendary fame. At a young eighteen, he had worn the triple collar bars of a captain in the Confederate States Army. Leading the Texas Light Cavalry's Company "O," he had played havoc with the Yankees in Arkansas and built a reputation equal to Dixie's other two daring military raiders, Turner Ashby and John Singleton Mosby.[1] Veterans of the Arkansas campaign boasted of his lightning-fast draw and deadly accurate shooting with the matched Colts, or about his uncanny skill when fighting with his bare hands. It was whispered that he had prevented an attempt by Unionist fanatics to stir up an Indian war which would have decimated much of Texas;[2] and had assisted Belle Boyd, the Rebel Spy, on two of her missions.[3] After the War had ended, he had hoped to resume his interrupted career. Fate had made him segundo of the great OD Connected ranch[4] and, again

---

[1]Told in *Under the Stars and Bars* and *Kill Dusty Fog!*
[2]Told in *The Devil Gun.*
[3]Told in *The Colt and the Sabre* and *The Rebel Spy.*
[4]Told in the *'The Paint'* episode of *The Fastest Gun in Texas.*

according to rumor, another turn of its wheel had sent him into Mexico on an assignment of considerable importance to the peace of the United States.[1] Having brought it off successfully, he and two members of his ranch's crew had come to help the Schell family gather horses to rebuild the OD Connected's *remuda*.

Dusty and Jeanie looked part of the scenery as they sat their horses on the slope about two miles north of the Guadalupe River's headwaters in Kerr County, Texas. The same did not apply to the third member of the party. Despite having acquired the high honor of being regarded as a .44 caliber man,[2] Colin Farquharson's appearance seemed better suited to a Scottish Highland deer forest.

Something over six feet in height, Colin had a muscular, powerful physique that went well with his ruggedly handsome features. A round, brimless bonnet rode at a jaunty angle on his brown hair, with an eagle's feather angled backwards from under the silver insignia of the Clan Farquharson at its left side. The tight-rolled blue bandana trailed its ends over a conventional, open-necked grey shirt such as might have been worn by any Texas cowhand. About his waist was strapped a Western-pattern gunbelt, with an ivory-handled Dragon Colt butt forward at the right side in a low cavalry twist draw holster. In a metal-tipped leather sheath at the left of the belt hung a long Scottish dirk with a thistle-shaped, finely carved wooden hilt and a double-edged, spear-pointed blade.

So far, apart from his bonnet, Colin conformed with the dictates of local fashion. Nothing else of his attire did. Under the gunbelt, extending to just above his bare knees, was a Farquharson tartan kilt. Thick woolen stockings of the same black, dark blue, deep green, check pattern, interspersed with red and yellow lines, covered his thick calves and disappeared into low-heeled, untanned boots. The hilt of a small, but deadly, *sgian-dubh* knife rose from the outside of the right stocking's top.

[1]Told in *The Ysabel Kid.*
[2]How Colin earned the name and what it implies is told in *.44 Caliber Man.*

While determined to remain and make Texas his permanent home, Colin still clung to some of the Highlander's traditional style of dress. He possessed sufficient physical strength and all-round fighting ability to make sure that his right to do so would be respected.

"Could be Lon coming back, Jeanie," Dusty commented. "Best make sure, though."

Dismounting, they allowed their horses' reins to dangle free and advanced up the slope on foot. Cautiously raising his head to peer over the rim, Colin pursed his trim-moustached lips in a silent whistle of admiration at what he saw in the valley beyond it. Dusty's insistence on making sure of what awaited them had paid off and Colin considered it worthwhile.

About forty horses were grazing in the valley; mares, foals, yearlings and maybe a dozen young stallions. All looked to be finely bred and in the peak of condition. Over the past weeks, Colin had seen many similar sights. The years of the War had allowed the bands of wild horses to build up their numbers, just as it had permitted the longhorn cattle to increase practically unchecked by human agencies. Some of the *manadas*—a Spanish word adapted to mean a bunch of mustangs—had been larger in number than this one, but none had exceeded it in the excellence of its members' conformation, especially among the younger animals.

"Colin!" Jeanie breathed, her left hand closing on his bulging right bicep and tightening as excitement put a vibrant thrill into her words. "That's Mogollon and his band!"

Instantly the Scot's interest increased. Ever since throwing in his lot with the Schell family, he had been hearing about the horse called Mogollon. The Clan Farquharson were noted for their knowledge of matters equestrian, but a man did not need to be an expert to recognize Mogollon. Even among the well-shaped members of its *manada*, the *manadero* stood out from all the others. Not even the largest of the immature stallions still tolerated by their sire came up to Mogollon in size.

The master stallion stood a full seventeen hands. Large at the shoe, concave in the sole, open at the heel, provided with a big, flexible frog, each hoof narrowed a little to the coronet. They were feet ideally suited to withstand the poundings and strains thrown upon them by carrying the *manadero's* mighty body. Above the coronets, the pasterns angled correctly, being neither too sloping nor too upright. Short in proportion to to the forearms, the cannon-bones gave the impression of a razor-like flatness. Long, not too horizontal forearms joined powerful, sloping shoulders which made the withers lie farther rearward than the elbows. While they did not "come out of the same hole," as mustangers expressed it, the front legs were close enough together to avoid giving a rolling, paddling[1] gait.

Short and strong of back, with the rib cage well sprung to give plenty of room for heart, lungs and other vital organs, it carried smoothly into long and slightly sloping hips. Designed as the major portions of the propulsion mechanism, the stifles had a muscular development that told of enormous power. Set high on the body, the tail arched and flowed proudly as Mogollon moved.

Of perfect proportions, the neck arched elegantly, being fine and flexible where it connected to the head at the poll. The head had an almost classical diamond configuration, with plenty of brain space above the eyes. Carried upright, the ears moved constantly to catch any warning sound. Set well out at the sides of the head, the eyes commanded a wide range of vision and glinted brightly with health. Although the face narrowed down at the muzzle, the jaws were wide at their junction with the neck, giving ample space for the windpipe. The lips closed firmly over the teeth and the nostrils, fine at the edges, flared open for easy respiration. Composed of perfectly straight hair, the forelock and mane were not particularly voluminous—hinting at a good bloodline—and swept down the left of the neck.

Glowing with health, rippling with steel-spring powerful muscles, the stallion's dark liver-colored chestnut hide

---

[1]Paddling: turning the hooves outward as they are raised to take a forward step.

carried a small white star in the center of its forehead and a white sock on each of its legs.

Watching the stallion as it stood grazing clear of the *manada*, with frequent pauses to search the surrounding area for danger to its band, one might have imagined that it had always been a free-ranging creature of the wild. Such was not the case. It had been brought into Texas as a war mount by one of a raiding Mogollon Apache band just before the War between the States. By the time its owner had been shot from its back, the big young horse had attracted much attention by its speed and endurance. Those qualities had been so effective that the rest of the war party could not catch the horse before being driven back to their own country by Jack Cureton's Company of Texas Rangers.

Since that time many stories had grown around the chestnut stallion left behind by the Apaches. Gaining control of a *manada*, it had not only held its growing harem against the other male horses but led them to safety through many attempts by human beings to trap them. Men had started speaking of it as "that Mogollon's horse," then shortened the name to Mogollon.

"So that's Mogollon, Jeanie," Dusty said. "I've heard your pappy talk about it. Curse it some too."

"He sure did," the girl agreed, looking at the *manadero* with longing eyes. "Pappy tried most every year, but even he couldn't lay hold of that Mogollon hoss. Each time Pappy would say, 'Never again,' but we'd always come back for another go."

"I can see why," Colin remarked. "Yon's a fine horse, lassie."

"Pappy allus had his heart set on taking Mogollon," Jeanie replied, her Texas drawl wistful and her fingers slackening their grip on Colin's arm. "Not to sell, though. He always allowed if we ever got him we'd keep him as a stud."

"He'd make a good one at that," the Scot confirmed, indicating the *manadero's* shapely offspring. "Look at the young ones he's sired."

"He leaves his mark on them for sure," Dusty drawled.

"Do you reckon we can take him, Jeanie?"

"If only we could!" the girl sighed. "Like I said, Pappy tried plenty of times and ways."

"With your ma, Mark and half the *mesteneros* off delivering the first of the Army's remounts to Fort Sawyer, we're a mite short-handed," Dusty went on. "But we could make a stab at it."

"He doesn't know we're around," Jeanie breathed, looking back the way she and the two men had come but failing to see any sign of the remainder of her family's Mexican assistants. "When Félix and the rest of the boys catch up with us, we might be—"

Before she could finish, Jeanie heard sounds across the valley. Swinging her gaze to the front, she noticed that Mogollon had also heard the noise. Pivoting around with the agility so sought in a cutting-horse, the stallion thrust up its head as far as its neck would allow and stared up the slope. Other members of the *manada* turned their attention in the same direction. Snorts broke from the horses and they moved around restlessly as they awaited their master's instructions.

With tails raised so the snow-white hairs flashed a warning, half-a-dozen buck whitetail deer appeared on the rim. They traveled at a fast gallop, instead of using the more usual canter interspersed by a succession of low leaps followed by a long, broad jump. That was a sure sign of an enemy close behind. Five of the band streaked down the slope in the direction of the horses. As the sixth buck topped the rim, the flat crack of a rifle shot sounded from behind it. Leaving the ground in a back-humping bound, the buck seemed to crumple in mid-air. It buckled forward, crashed to the earth on its side and slid lifeless down the incline for a few feet, then came to a stop.

Even before the shot rang out, Mogollon had decided that the deer heralded danger. So it cut loose with a commanding blast of a high-pitched whickering. Instantly the remainder of the *manada* started moving. Taking the lead, the two oldest mares set off along the bottom of the valley. After a swift swing of its shapely head, as if checking that all of its family had fled,

Mogollon strode along after them. Although clearly faster than the other horses, the big stallion made no attempt to go by them. Only rarely did a *manadero* lead its band in flight. Mostly it brought up the rear, holding the others bunched and urging on the laggards with snapping teeth. If the master stallion should decide that a change of direction was necessary, it would increase its speed until it caught the leaders and enforce its will with a ramming shoulder-thrust. With the line of flight altered to its satisfaction, it would drop back to its usual position.

"Wha—!" Jeanie gasped as the shooting of the deer speeded the hurried departure of the *manada*. "Who the—"

As if in answer to her question, the deer's killer crossed the rim. Smoke curled lazily from the rifle in his right hand and he sat afork a great white stallion with such relaxed grace that he might have been a part of it. The horse was fully as big, fine and wild-looking as Mogollon despite wearing bridle, bit, reins and a low-horned, double-girthed saddle as badges of servitude.

In a way the rider seemed to match his mount's untamed appearance. Around six feet in height, he had a lean, wiry build that spoke of endurance, agility and steel-spring resilience. Clad in cowhand clothing of all black, from his hat to his boots, he matched Colin's waist armament except that his Dragoon sported plain walnut grips and his knife was a genuine, ivory-hilted James Black bowie. Tanned to an almost Indian darkness, he had handsome features of nearly babyishly innocent aspect—except for his red-hazel eyes. They warned of his true, reckless, savage nature. Young he might look, but he rode and handled his rifle—one of the new model Henry's soon to be given the name Winchester '66—with casual competence beyond his apparent youth.

Throwing a glance after the fleeing horses, he dropped from his saddle by the buck's body. Then his gaze swung across the valley. Detecting Jeanie, Dusty and Colin as they started to rise, he raised his left hand in a cheery wave. Putting aside his intention of gutting and bleeding the buck, he went astride his white with a lithe bound and rode in the trio's direction.

"Blast you, Lon Ysabel!" Jeanie said indignantly as the dark-faced youngster approached. "You scared Mogollon off."

An expression of pained resignation crossed the newcomer's features and he raised his eyes to the heavens.

"You hear that, *Ka-Dih?*" the youngster demanded, mentioning the name of the Comanche Indians' Great Spirit. "There just ain't no pleasing white folks. 'See if you-all can bring in some pot-meat, Lon,' she said, afore witnesses for shame, 'n' when I do it, she starts to blister my hide." He looked at the girl and continued. "You sure it was me spooked them hosses, Jeanie-gal. Way you three was leaping up 'n' down, it could've been you's did it."

"Confounded Injun!" Jeanie snorted. "Trust you to try 'n' lay the blame on us white folks."

When the girl had called Loncey Dalton Ysabel an Indian, she had come very close to the truth.

Born in the village of the *Pehnane*—Wasp, Quick-Stinger, Raider—Comanches, the black-dressed youngster had been raised as a member of that hardy, fighting tribe. His mother had died giving birth to him and his father, a wild Irish-Kentuckian, had spent much time away from the village on the family business of smuggling. In the traditional Comanche fashion, it had fallen on the boy's maternal grandfather, Long Walker, a chief of the Dog Soldier war lodge, to educate him and the chief's French-Creole *pairaivo*—favourite wife—saw to his welfare.

Long Walker had carried out his work well.[1] By the time the boy had ridden off upon his first war trail, he was competent in all those matters a *Pehnane* brave-heart needed to know. Skilled beyond measure in matters equestrian, he could read and follow tracks barely visible to the eyes of less capable men. He had few peers in any race at locating hidden enemies and was equally adept at concealing himself from hostile eyes. He could handle a variety of weapons adequately and had attained prominence in the use of two kinds. With a rifle he could throw lead super-accurately under any conditions. His skill in

[1]Told in *Comanche*.

wielding a bowie had won him the Comanche man-name *Cuchilo*, the Knife.

All in all, the Ysabel Kid—as he had come to be known—had led a checkered life. Riding the smuggling trails with his father, he had learned lessons that were to be of use in later years. Although the Ysabels had enlisted in Mosby's Raiders, the Confederate States' Government had soon found a better use for their specialized talents. They had spent the remainder of the War delivering supplies, run into Matamoros through the U.S. Navy's blockade, across the Rio Grande into Texas. While carrying out those duties, the Kid had earned a reputation for being a real bad *hombre* to cross. Like Dusty, *Cabrito*—to give him the name spoken in awe by border Mexicans—had twice become involved in the affairs of the Rebel Spy.[1]

Bushwhack lead had ended Sam Ysabel's life and, while hunting for the killers, the Kid had met Dusty. In addition to avenging his father, the youngster had helped the small Texan to accomplish an important mission. With his quest ended, the Kid had decided that smuggling no longer interested him. So he had accepted Dusty's offer to join the OD Connected. Not as an ordinary cowhand, but as a member of the floating outfit, the elite of a tough and very capable crew. The larger ranches often made use of floating outfits, six or so top hands who roamed the more distant ranges instead of being based at the main buildings.

Along with another member of the floating outfit, Dusty and the Kid had been sent by Ole Devil Hardin to assist the Schells in gathering horses for the OD Connected's *remuda*. There were plans afoot to build up the war-ruined economy of Texas[2] and, to take full part in them, the ranch would need extra mounts for its hands. In addition to acquiring their own horses, Dusty, the Kid and Mark Counter were also helping the Schell family to fill an army remount contract. Their presence had been of

[1]Told in *The Bloody Border* and *Back to the Bloody Border*.
[2]How is told in *Goodnight's Dream* and *From Hide to Horn*.

the greatest use, especially as Colin Farquharson and Jeanie had earned the enmity of a murderous Mexican *bandido* family. That problem had been attended to, the first two hundred and fifty horses were on their way to the Army, and the remainder of the mustanging party headed to their next area of operations.

"Right sorry I scared off that *manada*, Jeanie-gal," grinned the Kid. "Anyways I saw another about three miles north of here. It's a *manada de hermanos*. About thirty of 'em, some good 'n's in it."

"There'll not be one to come up to Mogollan," Jeanie pointed out sadly.

Listening to the little girl who had captured his heart, Colin swore to himself that she would have the horse called Mogollon as his gift at their wedding. As Jeanie had claimed, the stallion would form a mighty sound base on which to found their bloodline when they quit mustanging and settled on a ranch to raise horses. Mainly, though, his wee Jeanie wanted Mogollon and that was all the inducement the young Scot needed.

With the blind impulsiveness of a young man in love, Colin gave small thought to the enormity of the task he set himself. While Félix Machado and the other *mesteneros* had taught him much about their trade, adding to his inherited flair for horse management, he could not pretend to know the mustanging business as thoroughly as had Jeanie's recently dead father.

If Trader Schell, rated by many as the best mustanger in Texas, had failed to find a way to capture Mogollon, it seemed unlikely that Colin could hope to do better. Yet the challenge of the situation aroused his fighting Scottish blood. Just as the knights of old went to perform difficult tasks to satisfy their ladies, so Colin intended to make the capture and training of Mogollon his quest.

Returning to his waiting horse, Colin silently swore by all the sacred oaths of the Clan Farquharson that Jeanie would own and ride Mogollon on the day she became his bride.

CHAPTER TWO

The man who had recently quit Béatrice, the Vicomtesse, de Brioude's bed was not her husband. Watching the door close hurriedly behind him, she smiled and rose languidly from the mattress which had served as a love—or lust—couch.

Five-foot eight in height, the Vicomtesse had a marvelous body. The black silk tights she drew on clung to her magnificently developed legs and hips like a second skin. Above them, her waist swooped in and her stomach showed not an ounce of surplus fat. Then her nacreous torso widened to accommodate two melon-like breasts which jutted forward so firmly that their nipples pointed to the front. Topping the voluptuous body, she had a full-lipped, sultry, beautiful face framed by shoulder-length black hair.

Directing her languorous gaze toward the door, Béatrice gave an annoyed sniff. Instead of concentrating on the pleasure at hand, her bedmate had spent the past hour worrying about the Vicomte coming and catching them, ignoring her repeated claim that Arnaud would never leave a card game until it ended. Taken with his inexperience—pathetically juvenile considering he was over twenty years old—1st Lieutenant Charles Lebel's concern that Arnaud would return had tended to make their liaison far less satisfactory than she had hoped. On being allowed to rise, he had hurriedly climbed into his uniform and almost fled from the hotel room.

Without adding to her attire, she crossed to the

window and looked down at the dusty, wheel-rutted main
street of Fort Sawyer. She liked little of what she saw.
Brownsville had been dull and boring enough, but her
present location was even worse. A chuckle broke from
her as she saw Lebel leave the hotel. With such a
French-sounding name, he ought to have been a far better
lover. Perhaps, as he was to command the de Brioudes'
military escort during their hunting expedition, she might
be able to help him improve his technique. Tall,
dark-haired, handsome, he had a fine, virile body under
his uniform. Certainly he was the best prospect of all the
men who would be accompanying herself and her
husband.

Watching Lebel cross the street, Béatrice chuckled
even more. He had drawn up and knotted his yellow
bandana to conceal the marks left on his neck by her
teeth. Then the chuckle died away as she noticed
something which jolted her attention from the young
officer.

"*Mon Dieu*!" breathed the Vicomtesse, but the tone
and the glow that sprang into her eyes was neither pious
nor reverent. "Now there is a *real* man."

Probably the same sentiments would have occurred to
the majority of women, even if they did not utter them
with such heart-felt vehemence and immediately start to
plan how to lure the man who had attracted the comment
into bed.

Striding by Lebel, the object of the Vicomtesse's
attention exceeded the lieutenant's six feet by a good three
inches. Under a white Stetson, its band decorated by
silver conchas, curly golden-blond hair topped a tanned,
classically handsome face. A tight-rolled blue silk
bandana dangled its long ends down a tan shirt that, like
his brown Levi's trousers, had been made to his measure.
That tremendously wide-shouldered, lean-waisted giant
frame could not have been clothed so perfectly from the
shelves of a general store. His trousers' legs hung outside
fancy-stitched, high-heeled boots produced by the same
masterly hands which had made his gunbelt. Of brown

leather, the latter carried a brace of ivory-handled Army Colts, in the fast-draw holsters tied low on his thighs.

Gripped in his left hand by its horn, a heavy range saddle bearing his bedroll, a coiled rope and a booted rifle, rested upon his right shoulder as if it weighed five rather than over fifty pounds. Eagerly Béatrice's eyes roamed over him, stripping away his clothing in her imagination and feasting her gaze on the immensely powerful body that must surely lie beneath them.

With a sense of ecstatic elation she observed that the blond giant was turning and walking toward the building in which she stood. For the first time since her arrival, she found herself regarding Fort Sawyer's finest hotel with something like favor. A dandy-dresser like that handsome blond would certainly make use of the place if he planned to stay in the town. Which meant that she would be saved the trouble of going to find him and could all the quicker come down to serious matters.

In a fever of eagerness, anticipation and excitement, Béatrice ran to the bed and started to dress. A glance in the dressing-table's mirror told her that she needed to give her face some attention. With the adjustments made, she slipped into a white silk blouse, feeling its cool embrace against her naked torso and leaving its flounced front open just a shade lower than could be termed decorous. A divided skirt of soft doeskin came next, ending just below the tops of her calf-high black riding boots. To emphasize the slender contours of her waist and set off her hips and bust to their best advantage, she drew tight the decorative silver buckle of a wide black leather belt. Deftly she adjusted a scarlet silk band about the rear of her head to hold her glossy hair tight behind her ears, then allow it to dangle loose on her shoulders. Finally she donned a pair of black leather riding gloves to hide her wedding ring from the blond's view.

Satisfied that she presented a picture no red-blooded man could ignore, Béatrice left her room. When the big blond failed to appear in the passage, she went down the stairs. Preparing to give a cough, or some equally attention-drawing sound, she came into sight of the entrance hall and its reception desk. What she saw brought her to a halt and tightened her full lips into angry lines. While she had been dressing, it appeared that another woman had beaten her to her quarry. Not, the Vicomtesse told herself, that the other would be a serious challenge as a rival.

Two inches shorter than Béatrice, and at least ten years older, the woman had shortish, curly blonde hair. If the Vicomtesse had been charitably inclined, she would have admitted that the other carried her age well. Her face was good-looking, showing strength of will and a sense of humour in its lines. Although firm-fleshed and without flabby fat, the gingham dress worn by the blonde did nothing to help her buxom figure.

Making sure that she did not come into sight of the desk, Béatrice listened to what was being said at it. Much to her delight, she saw the chubby, jovial clerk handing over two room keys, but his words robbed her of most of her pleasure.

"Seventeen for you, Mrs. Schell, and I'll put you in Fifteen, Mr. Counter."

While that placed the giant four doors from the de Brioudes' rooms, the buxom blonde would be between them. Béatrice's hope that the woman would be his mother ended and her thought that they might be strangers faded away.

"I saw you bringing them hosses in this morning," the clerk continued. "They looked a real fine bunch."

"Good enough," Mrs. Schell answered cheerfully. "What do you say, Mark?"

"Why sure, Libby," replied the blond giant, in a deep voice that sent shivers of anticipation through the listening Vicomtesse. "They're real good."

"Too good for a bunch of Yankee fly-slicers," sniffed the clerk.

"Maybe," Libby Schell said. "But they're paying cash money for 'em, 'stead of notes-of-hand on cattle that can't be sold 'cept for hide and tallow."

"Likely," admitted the clerk, knowing that the Schell family had supplied horses to more than one rancher who could only promise to pay in cattle. "Front!"

A bellhop darted from the rear of the building. Like almost every boy in Texas, he wanted to be a cowhand and could recognize a magnificent example of that hard-riding, hard-playing fraternity when one stood before him. So he studied Mark Counter with an air of hero-worship.

Although Mark would achieve considerable prominence as a member of Ole Devil Hardin's floating outfit, at that time he was practically unknown. During the War, he had been a 1st lieutenant in Bushrod Sheldon's cavalry and his taste in uniforms had brought him into conflict with numerous senior officers. He had gained a reputation as a peerless barehand fighter, possessed Herculean strength and could handle his matched Army Colts with considerable precision. Due to his being so much in Dusty Fog's company, he would never receive his full acclaim as a gun fighter. Dusty always declared that Mark ran him a close second in matters *pistolero*.

Son of a wealthy Big Bend ranch owner, Mark had helped Dusty and the Kid on the important mission in Mexico. Like the Kid, he had accepted the Rio Hondo gun wizard's offer of employment. Guessing that being a member of the floating outfit would offer opportunities for good companionship, fun and excitement, he had decided against going home. There were two older brothers at the R-over-C, so his presence would not be required. A top hand in all aspects of cattle work, Mark had proved an asset to the OD Connected.

Suddenly the bellhop's eyes swiveled from Mark to the stairs. Following the direction of the boy's gaze, Libby, Mark and the clerk looked to where Béatrice made her appearance. Ignoring the frank, adolescent scrutiny of the bellhop and the clerk's equally thorough study, the Vicomtesse made a hip-swiveling promenade to the desk. While she took pleasure in having males of any age looking at her with approval, she had bigger fish to fry. Directing a quick, suggestive glance from under her eyelashes at Mark, she turned her gaze to the clerk.

"Could you please tell me, *m'sieur*, if I can hire a horse to go riding?"

"Sure can, ma'am," the clerk replied, hardly able to tear his eyes from where Béatrice's nipples made twin hillocks against the material of the blouse. "Go to the livery barn across the street. You can't miss it."

"Will the horse be trustworthy, *m'sieur*?" the Vicomtesse continued, flashing a radiant smile at Mark. "I mean, one I can manage without difficulty."

If it was possible for five-foot eight inches of lascivious femininity to look and sound fragile, or in need of protection from the evils of the outside world, Béatrice came close to doing it. Unfortunately the clerk ruined the whole effect.

"How about your husband, ma'am?"

"My husband?" countered Béatrice, trying to make it sound like the clerk had made a mistake about her marital status.

Although he sensed that somehow he had said the wrong thing, the clerk went on, "Ain't he going riding with you, ma'am?"

Ever since the gorgeous woman had made her appearance, Libby Schell had been watching her. Studying the by-play without showing any noticeable interest in it, the blonde waited to see which way it was going. Despite having married young and spent much of her life roaming the Texas range country with her husband, she had acquired considerable knowledge of human nature. So she recognized Béatrice as being a walking man-trap and admitted that the beautiful foreigner was supplied with a perfect bait for the prey.

Libby glanced at Mark, guessing that he was the one Béatrice's words had been aimed at. Like the clerk and bellhop, the blond giant examined the newcomer with considerable enthusiasm.

"Well," Libby mused. "If Mark can't handle his-self around a married woman, he deserves all the grief he's likely to get."

"*M'sieur le Vicomte* has business matters to hold his

attention," Béatrice explained, the harsh timbre underlying the seductive tone telling Libby that the clerk's references to her husband had been unappreciated. "He cannot accompany me."

"Maybe Lieutenant Lebel'll be able to go with you?" suggested the man behind the desk. "He's only just left—"

"He has his duties to perform!" Béatrice gritted, for the clerk was going from bad to worse in his desire to be helpful. "I merely plan to take a short ride, if to do so will be safe."

"It sure will, happen you tell the owner to give you a steady hoss and don't go too far off, ma'am," answered the clerk. "Country hereabouts 's been real quiet since the Flores gang got wiped out by—"

"Hey, sonny," Libby put in, sensing that she and Mark might become involved in the conversation by virtue of their part in the "wiping out" of the Flores brothers' gang. "How about showing me to my room?"

"Huh?" grunted the boy, dragging his gaze reluctantly from the gently pulsating front of the white blouse. "Oh! Yeah! Sure thing, Mrs. Schell."

Bending over, the boy took hold of Libby's carpetbag and looked at Mark's saddle which lay alongside it. Although he raised the bag with no trouble, the bellhop faced a problem. One of his duties around the hotel was to carry the guests' baggage to their rooms. While a sturdy youngster, he knew that he would be hard-pressed to tote the saddle even without the added burden of the carpetbag.

"Best let me take that, *amigo*," drawled Mark and swung the saddle effortlessly on to his right shoulder.

Two sets of eyes followed Mark's actions, but with vastly different interests. The boy displayed admiration over the ease with which the blond giant hoisted up the load. Running the tip of her tongue across her lips, Béatrice contemplated the pleasures that might come her way if she played her cards correctly.

"Perhaps it would be better if I waited for an escort," the Vicomtesse purred and eyed Mark suggestively. "But I had so set my heart on taking a ride—"

When the big blond showed no sign of volunteering her services as the escort, Béatrice turned and made for the stairs. She went with an undulating gait that set her breasts bobbing and caused the cheeks of her rump to grind against each other in a fluid manner observable beneath her skirt. Eagerly the bellhop followed her and the new guests trailed along at a more leisurely pace. That was how Béatrice wanted things. Let *M'sieur le beau* Counter compare her with the fat old hag at his side and the Vicomtesse would find him the more susceptible on their next meeting.

"Whooee!" breathed Mark, watching Béatrice disappear into her room. "There goes a butt-end just begging for some feller to pinch it."

"Or for some gal to kick it," Libby said dryly. "Was I the clerk down there, I'd sure watch her 'n' her husband when it comes time for them to pull out."

"How come?" the big blond inquired.

Wishing to get a better view of the Vicomtesse's departing derrière, the bellhop had drawn ahead of Libby and Mark. So they carried on their conversation without being overheard.

"Happen her husband's too poorly off to buy her anything to go under that blouse," Libby elaborated, "he won't be able to pay his room rent."

"You mean she wasn't wearing *anything* under it?"

"Way you was a-sweating and staring down there, I figured you knew that."

"Can't say's how I noticed," Mark lied.

"Maybe the steam the clerk was raising fogged up your eyes same way it got on his spectacles," Libby grinned. "Was I you-all, I'd sure look under my bed afore you get into it tonight."

"I allus do," Mark assured her. "My Mammy taught me to have regular habits."

"This time you could find more than the chamber-pot there," warned Libby.

By that time they had reached the door of Room Seventeen and the bellhop opened it.

"Put my bag on the bed, son," Libby instructed, then

looked at Mark. "You feel like going riding?"

"Where d' you want to go?"

"Me?"

"Dusty said for me to stay close to you while you're toting the horse sale money," Mark reminded the smiling blonde. "And life goes a heap easier happen he's kept happy."

"I just thought you might want to take up that invitation you got down in the hall."

"Did I get one?" Mark asked in mock surprise. "Damned if *I* noticed it."

"Are you sure you're Big Rance Counter's son?" Libby demanded. "Anyway, after we've settled in, we'll go grab a meal. Then we'll collect the money and pay off the *mesteneros*—less you've other notions."

"Nary a notion, ma'am," grinned Mark and walked along to the door of his room.

Entering her quarters, Libby thought of the incident in the hall and smiled. That foreign gal had sure made her intentions toward Mark obvious. Given half a chance, she would have likely picked him up and toted him to her bed. Not that Libby entirely blamed her. Young Mark Counter was one helluva hunk of man.

"Now hush yourself from thinking things like that, Libby Schell," thought the blonde as the bellhop left the room. "And you not a year widowed, for shame."

After settling into their rooms, Libby and Mark went downstairs. Entering the dining room, which faced the bar on the other side of the hall, they found the Vicomtesse and a man they assumed to be her husband already present.

Tall, slender, dressed to the height of Eastern fashion, the Vicomte de Brioude had hair so thickly plastered with bay rum that it looked as glossy-black as his wife's. Although sallow and thin, his face was passably handsome. There was, however, an obsequious air about him that seemed more suited to a servant than a member of the *Ancien Régime*. For all that, everything about the couple's appearance hinted at considerable wealth and social standing.

Béatrice gave no sign of being aware of Mark's presence, other than darting an occasional glance his way. Libby had selected a table on the far side of the room and the meal went by without incident.

"That feller looked a mite peaked," Mark commented *sotto voce* after the de Brioudes had finished their meal and left. "Word around the hotel has it he's been playing poker most of yesterday and today. Could be that's what makes him look all tuckered out."

"Could be," Libby admitted. "How'd you find out?"

"Bellhop told me."

"The gal who turns down the beds allows they're real important folks back home in France," Libby remarked. "Come over here to hunt buffalo, antelope and the like. They'll be pulling out in a few days. Got them a hunter, skinner 'n' outfit. They've even fixed it to have an Army escort along."

"Likely been hearing how wild 'n' woolly Texas is," Mark grinned.

"Funny thing about that Countess," Libby said. "The gal allows she don't have a maid along."

"So?"

"So she packs and tends her things as neat as any maid."

"Maybe she's done a fair piece of traveling and had to learn."

"Or she *was* a maid and married the boss's son."

"You gals sure sharpen your claws on each other," Mark drawled.

"Yah!" Libby sniffed. "It wasn't *me* who learned about her husband being out all night playing poker."

"I didn't ask the boy," Mark objected. "He told me. What do we do now we've ate, Libby?"

"Go tend to business," Libby replied.

Leaving the hotel, Libby and Mark went to collect the payment for the two hundred and fifty horses. Then they made their way to the Mexican section of Fort Sawyer where the *mesteneros* were waiting to receive their money. With that matter attended to, they continued with a round of business and social calls which kept them occupied until sundown. From then until almost midnight, they joined in the *mesteneros'* celebrations.

Wherever the blonde and the big Texan went, curious eyes followed them. Already the whole town was buzzing with talk of how Libby Schell had sold a large bunch of horses—varying, depending on the source of the rumor, from the actual number to over two thousand—to the Yankee Army's buyer. People studied Libby with interest and some envy. On average, Colonel Monaltrie had paid twenty dollars a head for the remounts. That totaled up to a whole heap of money. Legal tender, too. Not like the Confederate States' currency with which most folks found themselves stuck at the cessation of hostilities. Few of Fort Sawyer's citizens could show an equal amount to that obtained by Libby and carried in a moneybelt about Mark's waist.

On the whole, however, the consensus of public opinion was that anybody with notions of relieving Libby of her money would wind up by regretting the idea. That big blond cowhand looked strong enough to break a man in two with his bare hands and his Colts hung just right for a real fast draw.

Shortly after midnight, following a hectic session of celebrating at the *Posada del Mesteneros*, Mark undressed to his long-handled underpants. With the moneybelt under his pillow and his gunbelt hung over the back of a chair so that he could reach the right hand Colt swiftly should the need arise, he climbed into bed. About five minutes went by and Mark was almost asleep when a faint clink drew his attention to the door. He had not bothered to draw the drapes and the light of the moon illuminated the door. The key he had turned and left in the lock now lay on the floor. Even as Mark sat up and slid the right hand Colt from its holster, he heard the lock click and saw the door start to open.

"If you-all after Libby's money," Mark mused, thumb resting on the long-barreled revolver's hammer-spur, "you've come to the right room—but a whole heap too early to catch me asleep."

CHAPTER THREE

Holding the Colt ready for use, Mark watched the door open and a figure enter. On the point of cocking and firing the revolver, he refrained from doing so and let out a hiss of surprise.

Clad in a diaphanous robe, left open to display an equally flimsy nightgown, the Vicomtesse de Brioude closed the door. Easing the robe from her shoulders in a tantalizing manner, she approached the bed with an air of concupiscence. Her whole attitude hinted that she expected Mark to greet her with open arms.

"What the hell?" Mark growled, sounding anything but delighted at the visit.

Suspecting that he might be running into the old badger game, Mark retained the Colt in his right hand as he swung his legs from and sat on the edge of the bed. If the woman's husband burst in, ready to demand payment for the "alienation" of his wife's affections, he would receive a response that might not be accorded to the male half of a "badger" team operating in Europe.

Unaware of the suspicions Mark harbored toward her, Béatrice tossed her robe on to the foot of the bed. Her eyes raked Mark from head to toe and she decided that, if anything, she had underestimated his physical attractions on first seeing him from her window.

"You shouldn't have sat up, *mon chérie*," Béatrice purred. "And you won't need that revolver."

Everything appeared to be going exactly as the Vicomtesse had planned it. Much to her annoyance, she had found no opportunity during the afternoon or evening to develop her acquaintance with the blond giant. If Arnaud had noticed her interest in Mark during lunch, he had given no hint of it. Flushed with success at having emerged a winner from the poker game, her husband had insisted on celebrating with an after-lunch session of lovemaking. While Béatrice never objected to *that*, she had had her heart set upon the change many philosophers insisted was as good as a rest. By the time Arnaud's passion had worn away and he returned to the poker game, *le beau* Counter and the fat old woman had left the hotel.

Learning that Mark would not be returning until late, Béatrice had made preparations. Waiting until she could do so unobserved, she had taken the hotel's passkey from its hook behind the reception desk. Having obtained the means to enter the Texan's room, she had returned to her quarters and changed into suitable attire for the occasion. Leaving her own door open an inch or so, she had settled down with what patience she could muster to await Mark's return. Time had dragged by slowly, but she had consoled herself with thoughts of the pleasure to come. Unless she misjudged her man, Béatrice expected a night to remember.

On hearing Libby and Mark arrive, Béatrice had watched them enter their respective rooms. Wise in such matters, she waited long enough for them both to undress and get into their beds. Then she had set out for her assignation. Using the passkey, she had gained admittance to Mark's quarters and—although she did not guess it—had come mighty close to taking a bullet in the head as she entered.

Now she was prepared to reap the benefits of her enterprise.

Unfortunately, she had reckoned without Mark's views on the matter. Maybe the big cowhand had an eye for a well-turned set of feminine curves and was not averse to dalliance with members of the opposite sex,[1] but there were limits to how far he would go. His interest in the

---

[1]This is proven in *Troubled Range* and *The Wildcats*.

Vicomtesse had departed the moment he had learned that she was married. So the sight of Béatrice in his room gave him none of the pleasure nor desire she had expected to arouse.

Ignoring the cooing words, Mark returned the Colt to its holster. He rose and strode toward Béatrice. Eyes glowing with lust and eagerness, she raised her hands ready to slip off the nightgown. Before she could touch the shoulder straps, Mark had caught hold of her arms. Drawing them together, he enfolded her wrists in his powerful left hand. Gathering up her robe with the right hand in passing, he started to haul her toward the door.

"What—?" Béatrice croaked, hardly able to believe that he planned to evict her. "Let go of me!"

"I sure as hell will," Mark promised grimly. "Just as soon's I've tossed you out of my room."

"You filthy pig!" the Vicomtesse spat viciously, her voice rising higher with each syllable. "You stinking Yankee pig! I came here to—"

Realizing that the woman would be screaming loud enough to wake up the other occupants of the building if she continued, Mark knew he must stop her. Tucking the robe into the waistband of his underpants, he whipped his right palm hard across her cheek. The force of the slap rocked her head violently to one side. Tears burst from her eyes and the pain of the impact brought her words to an abrupt end.

"Start yelling again and you'll get some more," the blond giant warned, ignoring the kicks she lashed at his legs and reaching for the door's handle. "I know why you came here and your husband's the man to give it to you."

"H-He-pl-plays-ca-cards with the sher-sheriff and oth-other men," the Vicomtesse sobbed, tears ruining her carefully applied make-up. She kept her voice down, guessing that the Texan would carry out his threat. "If-if-y-you-do as you-s-say, I'll g-go and t-tell them you tr-tried to f-force yourself on to me."

"I'll chance that," Mark growled, opening the door and thrusting her into the dimly lit passage.

Catching her balance and skidding to a halt, Béatrice

twisted around. Before she could speak or make another
movement, Mark had flung her robe into her face and
closed the door. By the time she had torn the clinging
fabric from her head, she had heard the click of the lock.
A string of violent French oaths bubbled furiously from
her lips, sounding all the more obscene coming from such
a beautiful set of features. She looked like a great wildcat
preparing to spring at and rend its prey with teeth and
claws. Pitching up and down with the force of her
emotions, the all but naked hemispheres of her bosom
seemed to throb with an inhuman passion.

For a moment she was on the verge of leaping at
Mark's door and battering it with her fists. Cold, savage
logic prevented her from doing so. With an almost visible
struggle, she calmed herself down. A vicious glint came to
her eyes as she remembered the things she had heard
about how Texans treated a man who molested a "good"
woman.

"You just wait, *le beau* Counter!" Béatrice hissed
audibly, taking hold of her nightgown and ripping it
down the front. "You'll pay for spurning me. See if you
don't, my friend."

Still sniffling and screwing her eyes up to make the
tears keep coming she scuttled to her room. Inside, she
rumpled her hitherto immaculate hair and donned a more
sedate robe. Scowling at her tear-stained face in the
mirror, she nodded her satisfaction. She looked just right
to arouse sympathy from her husband's poker-playing
companions and inflame their desire to avenge her
"besmirched" honor. Smiling in a manner that, taken
with the tears still trickling along her cheeks and her
disheveled appearance, made her look old and evil, she
returned to the passage. Throwing a glare of undistilled
hatred toward Mark's door, she made her way to the
room in which her husband was playing poker.

After locking his door, shoving the passkey out with
his own, Mark returned to the bed. He sat down and let
the anger ooze from him, then started to raise his feet
from the floor. Before he could lie down, he heard a soft

knock at the door. Flinging himself from the bed, he stamped grimly across the room.

"If that's you again—!" Mark began.

"It's not," Libby Schell's voice replied. "Open up, Mark!"

"What the—?"

"Do it. *Pronto!*"

"Let me put some clothes on first," Mark suggested, impressed by the note of urgency in the blonde's voice.

"There's no time for that!" Libby warned him. "Open up, damn it, or you're in real bad trouble."

Wondering what the woman meant, Mark obeyed. Certainly she would not act in such a manner for the reason that had brought the Vicomtesse to his door. Almost as soon as he had operated the lock, Libby twisted the handle and pushed her way in. Bare-footed and wearing a far less glamorous nightdress than Mark's last visitor, she looked like she had come to stay. She carried her dress, underclothing and shoes in her arms. In her right hand, she held the passkey by which Béatrice had entered.

"What's the idea, Lib—?" Mark began.

"Lock the door again," the blonde ordered, hurrying across the room.

Frowning and puzzled, Mark obeyed. On turning, he found that Libby had dumped all her clothes on the chair that held his own. Going to the window, she opened it and hurled the passkey along the alley behind the building. Closing the window again, she swung to face the big Texan.

"Get in bed," Libby said, voice tight with emotion. "We likely don't have much time if she's doing what I reckon she aims to."

"What—?" Mark gasped.

"Get in bed, damn it!" Libby hissed. "Do you reckon I'd be doing this if it wasn't necessary?"

"I don't—"

Once more Mark's words trailed off in surprise at Libby's actions. Wriggling out of her nightdress, she climbed into the bed as naked as the day she was born and threw the garment underneath. Seeing that Mark hesitated, her face twisted in an expression of anger. Realizing that only a most unusual and desperate set of circumstances would cause Libby to act in such a manner, Mark joined her in bed.

"Turn this way," Libby ordered as he lay on his back. "Damn it! This's no game I'm playing. That foreign hussy's planning mischief and us looking right might save you from a bad fuss."

Rolling on to his side and feeling her upper arm slip across his neck, Mark opened his mouth to ask for further details. Then he heard feet running along the passage and saw the glow of a lamp appear under the crack of the bottom of the door. Close against his, the firm, warm flesh of Libby's body was shivering. He realized what an ordeal it must be for her to be acting in such a brazen manner. His request for information went unsaid.

The feet halted outside Mark's door and a brief, muttered conversation followed. There was a sudden, violent crash and the lock sprang open to let the door burst inward. Two middle-sized, stocky men wearing the dress style of professional gamblers thrust into the room with revolvers in their hands. Behind them loomed the big, flabby form of Sheriff Lansing, the Vicomte and three more men.

Mark's reaction to the intrusion was immediate, instinctive and appeared completely natural under the circumstances. Sitting up, he jerked Libby erect with him. The bedclothes fell away, showing their naked torsos as Mark grabbed for his nearer revolver.

"What the hell—?" Mark spat out as the Colt left its holster and its hammer reared back under his thumb. "Ben Thompson!"

Coming to a halt, the gamblers stared across the room. After making sure that they had seen her state of undress, Libby left out an embarrassed screech and jerked the blankets up to her chin.

"Well I'll be—!" Ben Thompson ejaculated, letting his

revolver's barrel sag toward the floor. "Air that you, Mark?"

"Yeah," the blond giant confirmed. "What's the game, Ben, Billy?"

"It's a mistake," the older of the Thompson brothers replied and looked over his shoulder. "This here's Mark Counter, Arnaud. I know him real well. It couldn't've been him's tried to lay hands on your missus."

"It sure couldn't," grinned Billy Thompson.

"What's up, Ben?" Mark demanded, figuring that the question would be expected of him.

"The Count here's missus had some feller get into her room and try to ra-jum-well, you-all know what I mean," Ben Thompson answered. "Allowed it was the big jasper's has this room. We didn't know it was you in here, Mark."

"You're big all right," the gambling gun fighter's younger brother chuckled. "Only you sure as hell wouldn't be chasing no oth—"

"Shut your fool mouth, Bill!" Ben snapped. "'Scuse him, Mark, he's a fool kid who don't mean nothing—"

"Get out of here!" Libby shrieked.

"Has Mr. Counter been with you all night, Mrs. Schell?" Lansing inquired as the Thompson brothers turned to leave.

"He's been in here ever since we got back from the *Posada del Mesteneros*," Libby replied, telling the truth if not answering the question. "Now will you-all get the hell out of here and leave us have some sleep?"

"Come on, we've got the wrong man," Ben Thompson said, making for the door and holstering his Colt. He looked back and went on, "Right sorry to have bust in on you like this, ma'am. Damn it, Arnaud, that missus of your'n could've got us killed, saying what she did."

"I will speak to her about it," de Brioude promised, throwing a calculating glance into the room. His eyes rested on Mark for a moment. "I'm sorry if my wife has caused you inconvenience, *m'sieur*."

Leaving the bed, Mark turned the key of the "sprung" lock. He closed the door after the intruders and locked it.

Instead of rejoining Libby, he stayed and listened to the men talking in the passage.

"I never thought Libby Schell'd do nothing like that," Lansing commented.

"Was I you, I'd not go talking too much about it neither," advised Ben Thompson. "Mark Counter might not go for that and, mister, he's a man it's best not to have riled at you."

Which was not a bad tribute, coming from one of the fastest and most dangerous men in Texas. At that moment, though, Mark felt more grateful to Thompson for the warning he had given to the sheriff. If Lansing took it to heart, he might not spread the story of Libby Schell's indiscretion. Mark hoped that the affair would be finished, but his hope failed to materialize.

"You stop out here and keep watch on the Countess's room, Billy," Ben Thompson suggested. "The rest of us'll take a look around outside. Could be that feller's still around."

"He wants catching, whoever he is," declared one of the poker players, "abusing a for-real lady that ways."

"Maybe you'd best have one of your deputies come over and stand guard for the rest of the night, sheriff," Thompson continued.

"I will," Lansing agreed, always willing to oblige, or ingratiate himself, when dealing with influential visitors.

"If that feller was big enough for Arnaud's missus to mistake him for Mark Counter," Billy drawled, "I should have your man tote along a ten-gauge scattergun."

"It'd be best," Ben agreed. "Come on. Let's go look around."

"They've gone," Mark said, walking slowly back to the bed. "I don't know how you got in on the deal, Libby, but I'm surely grateful for what you've done."

"There wasn't any other way," the blonde replied. "I heard you and her fussing and figured to cut in. Time I'd got to my door, you'd thrown her out. Way she acted, I guessed what she aimed to do—"

"She said she'd go tell her husband I'd tried to make love to her, only I figured she was bluffing."

"I didn't. After she went into her room, I grabbed my clothes to make it look right and came here. Way you kept arguing, I was thinking she'd come out and see me. Boy, you're sure hard to get in to see."

"You called the play right, though," Mark said, wondering how to break the news of what he had heard in the passage.

"Sure," answered Libby. "They found us in bed, everything looking like we'd been there since we came in tonight. When they find the key in the alley, they'll reckon the 'feller' dropped it as he lit out."

"Likely," Mark replied.

Going to the window, the big blond looked out. After a short time, the lamp's light glowed and the men came into the alley. He saw one of them bend and pick up the key. Behind him, the bed's springs creaked. Turning, he saw Libby leaning over and reaching beneath it in an attempt to locate her discarded nightdress. Finding the garment, she sat up.

"What's happening?" Libby inquired, for Mark had swung back to the window.

"They've found the key and're looking around," Mark told her. "Libby, Billy Thompson's out in the passage right now and the sheriff's sending along one of his deputies to keep watch outside her door for the rest of the night."

"Which means I'll have to stay put," the woman said calmly. "If I go, they just might start figuring I only came in to save your hide."

"That'd be Lansing's kind of figuring, for sure," admitted Mark. "I'll bed down on the floor."

Libby did not comment straight away. Coming to Mark's rescue in such a manner had not been easy. Yet she had not been unaware of his rugged masculinity during the short time she had nestled against him. Never a promiscuous woman, she had been faithful to her husband through their years of marriage. However Trader had been dead for many months and she felt an urge to make love. Trader had always told her that she must live her life if anything happened to him and not tie herself to his memory. Sucking in a deep breath, she looked at the big Texan. Maybe a youngster like him would not wish to share a bed with a woman of her age.

"That's up to you," she said in a challenging manner.

"I figured you'd want it that way," Mark drawled.

"If word of this gets out," Libby remarked, "my name'll be ruined around town no matter where you sleep."

"Yes, ma'am," Mark agreed. "Which it'd be a real shame for that to happen."

"Hell, I don't care about it happening," Libby stated. "Not as long as I've done something to deserve it."

"In that case, ma'am," Mark said, taking the nightdress from her hands and placing it on the chair. "I'm right honored to be of service."

CHAPTER FOUR

Raising the chanter of a set of bagpipes to his lips, Colin Farquharson glanced to his right at the Ysabel Kid then left to Dusty Fog. They nodded their agreement and all turned their eyes toward the range ahead of them. Some thirty horses grazed on the grama grass about half a mile from the trio's place of concealment among a grove of post oaks. It was not Mogollon's band.

Much as Colin had hoped to commence his quest to catch the *manadero*, the band of mustangs located by the Kid had taken priority. It was a *manada de hermanos*, a band of brothers. In other words, a number of young stallions—not necessarily from the same sire—which had been driven from their original family groups by the jealous *manaderos* and had collected together for companionship or mutual protection. A *manada de hermanos* offered a larger return for effort than a *mestena*, a family band of mares and young horses. With luck, the majority of the stallions would be suitable for Army remounts, or to swell the number required by the OD Connected.

Knowing that Jeanie would go along with his wishes, the Scot had not mentioned his intentions regarding Mogollon. Instead, he had accompanied his companions to their base camp and spent the rest of the day preparing for the capture of the *manada de hermanos*.

After discussion with her *mesteneros*, Jeanie had decided that the stallions would be in the vicinity of the *Caracol* de Santa Bárbara. So the men had ridden to that enclosure—every major trap had a name—and made preparations for the *corrida* which, they hoped, would drive the *manada* into the figure-8 formation of the sturdy log walls.

Experience had taught mustangers that the ordinary circular type of corral did not meet their requirements when gathering in a large bunch of horses. So the gourd or *caracol*, snail-shaped, enclosure had come into being. Either of them prevented the horses from doubling back out of the gate as frequently happened when a round or lane pen was used.

Selecting the location of a catch enclosure was of considerable importance. In preference, it would be on the bank of a creek at a point where horses regularly crossed. Failing that, wood- or scrub-covered hollows, or canyons with sides the horses could not climb served equally well. If possible, the entrance would face the direction from which the wind blew with the greatest regularity. Given a wind that blew toward the corral, the dust stirred up by the *manada* would roll ahead of them and partially obscure the entrance until it was too late to be avoided.

With the *Caracol* de Santa Bárbara and its surroundings made ready, Jeanie had laid her plans for the *corrida*. All the party had known that enforcing their will upon the mustangs would be anything but easy. More than on any other *corrida* dealing with a *manada de hermanos* called for concerted action on the part of all concerned—and not a little luck.

The Kid had warned that one of the stallions was acting as *manadero*, which did not surprise his audience. Even after it had been driven from its position of leadership by a stronger rival, a deposed master-stallion would try to take over another band. Failing to gather mares, the ex-*manadero* would join a bachelor group. Like all herd-living animals, horses maintained an orderly society in which every individual knew and, unless it could improve its station by physical means, kept its place. So, as long as its strength held out, the retired *manadero* would often dominate its companions.

Unfortunately, the domination of *manadero* managed

to establish over a *manada de hermanos* was never as strong as upon the members of a *mestena*. Although generally subservient to their leader's will, once fright set them to running, the stallions would scatter more readily than the mares and offspring of a *mestena*.

With that in mind and being short-handed, Jeanie had utilized her small force in a manner which had brought nods of approval from the listening men. When they had ridden out at dawn on the day after seeing Mogollon, every man knew the part he must play in the work ahead of them.

No domesticated horse, burdened by a rider, could hope to run down and catch healthy, unencumbered mustangs, but they had to travel fast over a long distance. So no extra weight could be carried. Instead of using a heavy range saddle, each of the party sat on a sheepskin pad held in place by a single girth to which was attached the leathers of plain brass stirrups. The whole rig weighed a little over three pounds. To further reduce the horse's load, a hackamore with a bosal and reins replaced the full bridle and metal bit. While light and serviceable, such an outfit demanded a high standard of horsemanship from its user.

Accompanied by Dusty and the Kid, Colin had circled the area in which the *manada* was grazing. The Scot had a special and important part to play in the *corrida*. Early in his association with the Schell family, it had been discovered that the music of a set of bagpipes—brought to Texas for a kinsman but so far undelivered—produced an adverse effect upon horses unused to the sound. That aversion had been put to good use in starting the *manadas* moving.

"Go to it, *amigo*," Dusty suggested, controlling the eagerness of the small *bayo-cebrunos*[1] gelding he had selected instead of using his paint stallion that day. "Start up that caterwauling and let's see if we can get them headed the way we want them to go."

Holding down his inclination to defend his native

[1]Bayo-cebrunos: a dun merging into a smokey-grey color.

music, Colin started to blow into the chanter's mouthpiece and the skirl of the pipes rose hauntingly. On hearing the alien sound, the horses in the *manada* swung to face it. So far they were not frightened, for it came from a sufficient distance to pose no threat. However they paced restlessly, heads tossing and ears pointing toward the trees. Letting out an explosive snort, the big black *manadero* advanced a few steps in an attempt to form a better impression of what was causing the droning, wailing noise. Although a fair way past its prime, the stallion still looked menacing and savage.

"He's a mean one," drawled the Kid. "Just look at that off ear. It's damned near been chewed off his head."

"That's one horse we'll be lucky to take alive," Dusty answered, studying the tattered ear and scarred body. "And he'll be damned little use if we do."

"They're moving off," the Kid said.

While not frightened, the *manada* had clearly decided that they did not care for the strange noise. So they loped off without haste, going in the direction of the valley which held the *Caracol* de Santa Bárbara concealed in a draw.

"Just like Jeanie figured," Dusty drawled. "That gal's a living wonder at mustanging. Let's show ourselves."

Curiosity compelled first one then another of the *manada* to swing around and look at the post-oaks. Seeing the three riders appear, they cut loose with snorts of real alarm. This was no strange, but possibly harmless sound, it was a genuine menace. More of the *manada* turned, studying the human beings. Then the *manadero* let out an ear-shattering whinny. Twirling around fast, the horses which had been looking at the approaching riders joined their companions in flight.

"Now!" Dusty snapped, giving the *bayo-cebrunos* a heel signal which changed its walk to a gallop.

"Yeeah!" screeched the Kid and his strawberry-roan increased its pace.

A quick thrust turned the bagpipes to hang by their cord behind Colin's back. Knowing what would be required of it, the wolf-grey *bayo-lobo* horse between his legs sprang forward to keep level with the Texans' mounts.

Forming a wide, crescent-shaped line, Dusty, Colin and the Kid followed the departing *manada*. Each of them kept up his whooping, to urge the mustangs onward and alert the other members of their party that the *corrida* had begun. Striding out at speed, none of the stallions showed signs of separating from the remainder of the band. The black *manadero* brought up the rear, snaking its neck around occasionally to look at the pursuing men.

On reaching the edge of the valley, the horses plunged unhesitatingly down its gentle side. Laying flat along the neck of her quivering, impatient brown gelding, so as to remain hidden among a clump of mesquite, Jeanie watched them. When the leaders started across the level ground, she sent the horse bounding from cover.

"Cárn na cuimhne!" the girl shrieked, giving the rallying call of the Clan Farquharson, "Cairn of Remembrance," in honor of her fiancé, once more producing a satisfactory start to a *corrida*.

Gripping a saddle-blanket in her left hand, Jeanie waved and flapped it over her head. The girl's sudden and noisy appearance caused the leading stallions to swerve hurriedly in the required direction along the valley. Some of the following horses showed signs of breaking away and heading up the opposite slope. Placed there to circumvent such tactics, a *mestenero* called Bernardo appeared on the rim and rode in the deserters' direction. Turning back, the would-be bunch-quitters rejoined the *manada* to obtain mutual protection from its numbers.

Hooves rumbled and drummed in a growing crescendo, punctuated by the wild yells of the riders. Turned along the valley in the direction of the fatal draw, the *manada* was kept on the move by the girl and her companions. While the Kid rode parallel to the rim down which the mustangs had entered the valley, Bernardo remained on the other ridge. Dusty and Colin joined Jeanie on the bottom, urging their horses onward in an attempt to keep pace with the girl. Being smaller and lighter, Jeanie had the advantage over both of them.

Knowing the dangers involved in making a *corrida* on a *manada de hermanos*, the girl tried to restrain the brown gelding's eagerness. Despite all her efforts, she drew ahead as the chase continued. Nor could Colin stay level with Dusty, and the three riders formed an angular line across the valley.

Almost half a mile fell behind the pursued and the pursuers. Underfoot, the springy grama grass grew in such profusion that it prevented the dust from rising beneath the pounding hooves. Still in the lead of the trio, Jeanie regarded that as a mixed blessing. While it allowed her an almost unrestricted view of what lay ahead, the same also applied to the members of the *manada*. Holding her gelding to its racing gait, Jeanie could see the mouth of the draw which held the *caracol*. Beyond the opening, the yard-wide furrow dug by the *mesteneros* stretched across the valley and up the opposite slope.

Jeanie knew that the next few seconds would be of vital importance. The result of the *corrida* depended on what happened during them. While wild horses for some reason fought shy of crossing a naked strip of earth like the furrow, the response of a *manada de hermanos* to such a sight was far less predictable than that of a *mestena*. When they reached the furrow, the stallions might decide to scatter instead of turning as a band. If so, they would burst apart like an exploding canister shell spraying out its load of cast-iron balls. Then the whole band might be lost, or only a fraction of it fall into the *mesteneros'* hands.

At the sight of the furrow, the leading stallions of the *manada* started to swing aside—but not toward the entrance of the trap. Positioned to counter such an eventuality, Jeanie's segundo, Félix Machado and another *mestenero* made a sudden and rowdy appearance on top of the slope up which the stallions were heading. Yelling and waving blankets, they charged toward the *manada*.

Watching the whooping, hard-riding pair approach the stallions, Jeanie caught her breath in anxiety. Knowing what must be done, she directed her fast-moving mount toward the edge of the incline down which

Félix and Carlos were making their reckless descent. Equally aware of the danger, Dusty continued to hold his *bayo-cebrunos* in the center of the valley and about thirty feet to the girl's rear. Approximately the same distance behind Dusty, Colin steered his *bayo-lobo* along the foot of the other slope. Confronted by Félix and Carlos, the stallions skidded into rump-scraping, hoof-churning turns. At that moment, everything swung on a very delicate balance.

"Yeeah!" Dusty bellowed, giving the start of the battle cry which with its accompaniment of "Texas Light!" had been so well known and hated by the Yankee soldiers in Arkansas.

"Cárn na cuimhne!" Jeanie screeched, voice hoarse and cracked from its earlier efforts.

"Cárn na cuimhne!" echoed Colin, the wild excitement of the chase stirring his Highland blood and adding a ringing turbulence to his utterance of the clan's slogan.

Approached on two sides by the yelling, hated man-creatures, faced by that mysterious—therefore dangerous and to be avoided—strip of bare ground on the third, the *manada* was left with only one way to go. Wild-eyed, tails streaming in the breeze, the stallions still retained sufficient of their herding instincts to hold together as they plunged toward the "safety" offered by the mouth of the draw.

Only the old *manadero* saw the danger. Swinging away just before it reached the entrance, the big stallion gave a spine-chilling scream and charged at the nearest of its pursuers. Head thrust forward to the full extent of its out-stretched neck, eyes rolling, ears laid flat back and mouth open to display worn-down, age-yellowed teeth, mane bristling furiously and tail spiked straight to the rear, it made a frightening picture.

Certainly Dusty's *bayo-cebrunos* gelding thought so, for it had been the animal selected by the black *manadero* to be attacked. While it was now a trained cow-horse, the *bayo-cebrunos* had begun its life in a wild *mestena*. During its formative years, it had experienced the domination of a master-stallion. No other creature, except possibly man, exercized such a complete despotic rule over its offspring. So the *bayo-cebrunos*, which would face the charge of a hostile longhorn bull without flinching, showed the greatest reluctance to going up against the *manadero*.

Throwing back its head, the little horse attempted to come to a stop and turn away all in one motion. Dusty felt its feet slipping from under it as it lost its balance. If he had been afork his own saddle, the small Texan might have averted the trouble. The ultra-light rig, combined with the noseband bosal instead of a bit did not allow him to exert the necessary control with his hands or legs.

Feeling the *bayo-cebrunos* going down and knowing that he could not prevent it, Dusty snatched his right boot from the brass stirrup "iron." The horse was falling that way and he had no desire to be trapped beneath it. Swinging his leg forward and over the gelding's neck, he kept his other foot in the stirrup to give him support. When the time came to remove it, he felt his boot cling in the grasp of the brass semi-circle.

A sudden jerk ripped Dusty's foot free, but his equilibrium had been destroyed. Instead of landing running as he had planned, he stumbled and went down. Long experience at riding bucking horses had taught him how to fall, even unexpectedly, with the minimum of pain or chance of injuring himself. Ducking his head forward and twisting his torso, he landed on his left shoulder with his body curled into a ball. Rolling over and over on the grama grass, he knew that he was still far from out of danger.

Shattering the air with its fighting screams, the raging *manadero* charged at the *bayo-cebrunos* and ignored Dusty. It almost seemed that the stallion intended to inflict punishment on the fallen horse for its betrayal of their species to the hated human beings. Rearing high on its hind legs, the black flailed its fore feet ready to smash down its hooves upon the helpless little gelding's body.

Knowing that there was only one way to deal with a kill-crazy *manadero*, Dusty prepared to do it—if he could. Ending his roll flat on his back, he sent his left hand flashing across to close on and draw the right side Colt. Even as the revolver's seven-and-a-half-inch barrel cleared leather, with his forefinger entering the trigger-guard and thumb easing back the hammer to full cock, he doubted if it possessed the power to halt the stallion in time to save his mount.

The 1860 Army Colt's twenty-five grain powder charge and .44 caliber, 212-grain bullet might be effective man-stoppers, but they lacked the energy to fell the horse instantly unless striking a vital spot. Under the circumstances, Dusty lacked the time needed to take a careful aim and ensure he hit such a spot. To merely wound the *manadero* could easily bring its attention and rage on to him, but he had to take that chance. Flat on his back, lining his Colt above his raised knees, he squeezed the trigger and directed his bullet at the *manadero's* ribs. Being hit there might turn the stallion and allow the struggling *bayo-cebrunos* to regain its feet and escape.

Although Dusty did not know it, help was already coming. Seeing the small Texan's perilous predicament, Colin acted with speed, decision and purpose. Twisting his right hand palm outward, he swept the big old Dragoon from its holster. Back reared the hammer beneath his thumb and he thrust the sixty-five-ounce revolver to arm's length. Looking along its round barrel almost as if sighting a shotgun, the Scot tightened his forefinger on the trigger.

Two seconds after Colin's hand had closed on the ivory butt, flame spurted from a percussion cap. In the uppermost chamber of the cylinder, forty grains of best du Pont powder turned into gases, which drove a conical .44, 219-grain soft lead bullet along the barrel's rifling grooves. Until improvements in steel made possible the use of the mighty .44 Magnum cartridge, no handgun would exceed the power of the 1848 Colt Draggon revolver when loaded to its maximum capacity.

Hurling through the air at a velocity of nine hundred feet-per-second, Colin's bullet struck the side of the stallion's throat an instant after Dusty's lead found its rib-cage. Ploughing through flesh and muscles, the

Dragoon's load broke the *manadero's* neck and crumpled it almost immediately to the ground.

Seeing its assailant falling toward it, the *bayo-cebrunos* screamed in terror. With legs waving wildly, it rolled on to its back. Keeping turning, it avoided being struck by the stallion's collapsing body. Then it lurched to its feet and went plunging off in the direction from which it had come.

"Catch my saddle!" Dusty yelled, sitting up and making the usual request given by a man who had been thrown and saw his horse bolting.[1]

"No time the now, laddie," Colin replied, hostering his Dragoon and grinning at the small Texan as his *bayo-lobo* carried him by. "There's work to be done—and money to be earned."

"Blasted foreigner!" Dusty bellowed in simulated anger after the Scot's departing back. "I always heard you jaspers from Scotland were mean."

As Dusty and Colin knew, the loss of the gelding would only be temporary. In fact the long, split-ended reins trailing about its fore legs had already begun to slow its flight. Trained to stand still when the reins dangled free, a precaution against the rider having to dismount and leave the horse in a location which offered no means of tying it up, the *bayo-cebrunos* did not go far before it came to a halt. Snorting and tossing its head, it made no further attempt to run away.

After watching his companions follow the remainder of the *manada* into the draw, Dusty walked toward his horse. He caught it without difficulty and, after calming it down, examined it. Finding it lathered, shivering a little, but otherwise unharmed, he took its reins and led it along the valley to rejoin the rest of the mustanging party.

Ignoring the departure of their leader, the stallions entered and ran along the sheer-sided draw toward the

---

[1] While the horse rode very often belonged to his employer, the saddle was always the cowhand's personal property. It was such a vitally important item of his equipment that its loss must be prevented if possible.

gate of the *caracol*. Urging them on, Jeanie watched anxiously. Always the actual entry into the enclosure was a tricky, chancy business. Let the mustangs receive just one hint of their danger and no power on earth could force them inside. However, the young stallions did not hesitate. Going by the disguised gate, they penetrated the forward action of the pen.

As soon as all the *manada* had entered the *caracol*, the last of the *mesteñeros* who could be spared to take part in the *corrida* made his appearance. He had been hidden behind the gate, ready to turn back any of the mustangs that tried to escape before it had been closed. Sliding their horses to a halt, Félix and Carlos helped the *mestenero* to swing the gate shut. Having watched the successful conclusion of their efforts, Jeanie twisted on her saddle and looked back along the draw.

"Is Dusty all right?" the girl inquired as Colin joined her.

"Aye, lassie," Colin replied, "but I had to shoot yon *manadero*."

"It happens," Jeanie said philosophically, and dismounted. Seeing the concern on her fiancé's face, she continued, "Don't feel bad about it, Colin. It was a quicker end than he'd've got had he escaped. He'd likely've been kicked to death, or crippled up bad, trying to get in on another *manada*. Or he'd get so all-fired old 'n' slow that the wolves or coyotes'd eat him alive."

"That's true enough," Colin admitted. "There's no pity for the old in the wild, lassie."

"We got the others, anyways," Jeanie enthused. "You've seen how often we have to shoot a *manadero*."

"I have," Colin said soberly.

It was one of the points he would have to keep constantly in mind when he started his hunt for the horse called Mogollon.

CHAPTER FIVE

Gripping a sack of potatoes by its neck and bottom in front of him, Mark Counter raised it from the floor. Libby watched him with admiration as he carried it toward the front door of Hoffer's general store. Despite having taken part in a most satisfying session of lovemaking, which had left them little time to sleep, he toted his hundred-weight burden with no more apparent effort than if it had been a five-pound bag of sugar.

Libby felt no regrets at her decision of the previous night. In the morning, after the deputy had gone from his guard duty outside the de Brioudes' room, Libby had dressed and returned to her own quarters. Ben Thompson had joined the blonde and Mark while they ate breakfast in the dining room. Making no reference to how he had discovered them the previous night, Thompson had told them what had happened following his departure from their presence. There had been little that they did not alreay know. On finding the passkey in the alley, Thompson's party had drawn the conclusions predicted by Libby. They had searched the surrounding area without locating any trace of the man responsible for the "attack" on the Vicomtesse. Although neither Mark nor Libby commented on the matter, Thompson's last piece of news had not surprised them.

Before they had finished their breakfasts, the Vicomte had arrived. Stiffly, in a manner coldly polite, he had apologized for the inconvenience his wife's "mistake" had caused to Mark. The Vicomtesse had not accompanied

44

him to breakfast, de Brioude had explained, because she had not yet recovered from her fright.

Taken all in all, Mark had felt relieved by Béatrice's absence. Not through any sense of guilt, but because Libby had threatened to hand-scalp the foreign woman the next time they met. While Mark had doubted if Libby would have deliberately started a brawl in public, a chance wrong comment from the Vicomtesse might easily have provoked an unpleasant incident.

With the meal over, Libby and Mark had collected their belongings from the rooms. Picking up her wagon, they had brought it to Hoffer's store. None of the *mesteneros* had made an appearance, so Mark started the loading.

As Mark was stepping out of the door carrying the sack of potatoes, he saw a big, thick-set, crop-haired United States Cavalry sergeant standing in the center of the sidewalk between him and the Schell family's wagon. At the same moment, Mark became aware that an equally hefty Yankee soldier was lounging just a mite too casually at either side of the entrance to the building.

"Mind moving aside, friend?" Mark inquired, making a reasonable request as the sergeant blocked his access to the rear end of the wagon.

"Walk 'round me, beef-head," was the cold, uncompromising reply.

Instantly Mark sensed danger. Having completed his packing quicker than Libby, he had gone downstairs to wait in the hotel's reception hall. While there, he had seen that same hard-faced sergeant in the dining room with the Vicomtesse de Brioude. At the time, Mark had sensed by their behavior that he was the subject of their conversation. The sergeant had scowled Mark's way and made as if to rise, but Béatrice had restrained him.

Being curious, Mark had taken the opportunity to question the desk clerk about the soldier. He had learned that Sergeant Heaps was the second-in-command of the de Brioudes' escort. Darting a worried glance at the dining room's door, the clerk had also intimated that he thought the couple had made a bad choice. According to him, the noncom had a reputation for being a bully and a troublemaker.

Studying the sullen, brutal face, Mark concluded that Heaps's reputation might be justified. He also wondered if the Vicomtesse had encouraged the sergeant to pick a fight as a means of taking her revenge. That seemed likely. After the failure of her first attempt to repay him for spurning her advances, a woman as vindictive as she had proved to be would hardly forget the matter so easily. If Mark had called the play correctly, he knew that there would be no evading the issue. Satisfied that trouble could not be avoided, he continued to advance without giving a hint of his suspicions.

Swinging toward Mark, the red-haired private at the left side of the door thrust forward his right leg. Acting as if he had seen nothing, Mark suddenly swung up and hurled the sack at Heaps. Already moving forward to the attack, the sergeant took the heavy weight full in the chest. Its impact knocked him across the sidewalk until a collision with the body of Libby's wagon ended his involuntary retreat.

Instead of being thrown off balance by the redhead's leg, Mark caught his weight on his forward foot and remained erect. Swinging his other leg around, he pivoted and flung a back-hand blow at the center of his assailant's face. Pain blasted through the redhead as hard knuckles crushed his nose. Yelping in torment, the soldier went spinning and teetering helplessly away from what the trio had originally regarded as an easy victim.

Like Sergeant Heaps and "Red" Going, Dip Noris had taken Mark for a wealthy young dandy who would be unlikely to put up a strenuous resistance while they earned the "Countess's" monetary gratitude. So Noris shared with his companions a sense of overconfidence and it brought him just as much grief. Mark was what he appeared, but with one major discrepancy. Instead of being soft and weak from easy living, he possessed a muscular development superior to any of his attackers and had been well trained in all aspects of roughhouse self-defense.

Catching hold of Mark's left shoulder, Noris prepared to jerk him around and drive a punch into his face. Maybe the beef-head had been fortunate against Red and Heaps, but Noris figured that his luck had about run out. Mark had other, definite ideas on the subject. Moving to the rear instead of trying to draw away from the clutching fingers, the blond giant propelled his right elbow behind him. It rammed with considerable force into Noris's *solar plexus*, causing him to gasp, remove his hand and retreat hurriedly. Nor had Mark finished with him. Turning around, the Texan hurled out his left fist. Bunched knuckles rammed into Noris's chest before the pain of the first attack could fold him over. After appearing to be running backward, the soldier sat down hard on the unyielding planks of the sidewalk.

Heaps allowed the sack to tumble unheeded to his feet. Sucking in a deep breath, he sprang over it. Advancing fast, he enfolded Mark's torso and biceps with his arms from the rear. Locking on a grip that no man had ever managed to break, the sergeant let out a bellow to his two assistants.

"Going! Noris! Get the hell here and help me!"

Before he had reached the fifth word of his demand, Heaps began to get an uneasy feeling that he really did need help. Under that excellently tailored shirt's sleeves bulged mounds of bicep mucles in excess of his own. Keeping his head held back to avoid being butted with the base of Mark's skull, he clung on grimly and a timbre of urgency crept into the remainder of his speech.

Taking his hands from his throbbing nose, Red Going stared for a moment at the blood on his palms. Then he turned his eyes to the man who had dealt him the injury. What he saw filled him with delight, for it offered the opportunity of returning the Texan's blow without too much danger. Trapped from behind in Heaps's vice-like bear hug, the efficiency of which Going had been demonstrated many times, the blond giant faced toward the wall of the store. So the burly redhead decided that he could safely approach and launch his attack.

"Hold him, Heaps!" Going brawled. "I'm coming!"

Shouting out his intentions proved to be an error in tactics, although the heavy thumping of his boots on the sidewalk would have warned Mark of the danger. Hearing Going approaching, Mark exerted all his strength in a way neither the redhead nor the sergeant expected. Mark knew that he could not break the noncom's hold quickly enough to be of use, so did not try. Instead, he gave a surging twist that turned him toward his second attacker.

Driving down with his feet, Mark took three long strides to meet Going and dragged the amazed Heaps after him. An experienced barroom brawler, Going could sense what was coming next even though he reacted too slowly to avert it. Balancing on his right leg, Mark lashed up his left foot in a wicked kick. Unable to stop his forward impetus, Going took the toe of the riding boot in his groin. The pain caused to the redhead's nose paled into nothing alongside the white-hot, nauseating agony which now blazed through him. Screaming and clutching at the stricken area, Going spun on his heels. Then he stumbled away, dropping to his knees and pitching face forward into the vomit which burst from his mouth.

Being a loyal subordinate—or, at least, aware of his fate if he stayed out of the fight—Noris prepared to return to the fray. To reach the combatants, he had to pass in front of the open door of the store. Although he saw Libby at it, he ignored her. Clenching his fists, he advanced along the sidewalk and watched Going rendered *hors de combat*.

On hearing the commotion, Libby had come to investigate. While she did not know what had started the fight, she could see enough to tell her that Mark might be needing some help. With that in mind, she hitched up her skirt and injected a bare, shapely leg between Noris's feet. Doing so might have been a repetition of the trick Going had tried on the blond giant, but there was one major difference. Mark had suspected that the attempt would be made and was ready for it. Libby's intervention took Noris completely unawares. Catching his rear foot against the woman's calf, the soldier went stumbling helplessly by Mark and Heaps to end his progress by falling over Going's recumbent body.

Taken with his earlier anxieties, the sight of his second helper blundering off uncontrollably caused Heaps to slacken his grip a little. Surging apart his elbows, Mark forced Heaps's arms to slip up to his shoulders. Catching the sergeant's right wrist with his left hand so that his arm also pinned the other's left forearm against the chest of the tan-colored shirt, Mark continued with his escape. Bowing his torso forward and forcing Heaps to duplicate the movement, Mark bent his knees and twisted to the left. By ducking his head forward and straightening his legs, he catapulted the sergeant over the upper part of his back. With Heaps in full flight, and feeling the blue-clad arms release their hold, Mark set him free. A small crowd of civilians had been attracted by the fight. While none of them had offered to intervene on Mark's behalf, they clearly appreciated the manner in which he dealt with the sergeant.

A trained cavalryman, Heaps managed to lessen the force of his landing on the wooden boards. He lit down rolling and came to a halt by the wall of the store. Thrusting himself on to his knees, he snarled a curse and started to knock open the flap of his holster.

Down flashed Mark's right hand, lifting its Colt from the holster in a flickering blur of movement. Cocking back the hammer and depressing the trigger *after* the gun had cleared leather and pointed away from him, Mark leveled the eight-inch barrel by instinctive alignment. Up so close, that method offered almost as much accuracy as taking sight in the formal manner.

Heaps would never be closer to death than at that moment.

Little more than a year had elapsed since the meeting at the Appomattox Court House had brought an end to the War between the States. For almost two years before that, the sight of a Union-blue uniform had nearly always meant shooting to the blond giant. Only by an effort of will did Mark refrain from bringing his draw to its ultimate conclusion by removing his thumb from the hammer's spur. If he had done so, the hammer would have flashed forward, struck and ignited the waiting percussion cap, detonated the powder charge and sent a bullet to tear its way into the sergeant's skull.

"Get your hand off it, *hombre*!" Mark ordered.

Concentrating on preventing Heaps's attempt to pull a gun, Mark did not see Noris preparing to rejoin the fight. Writhing clear of the moaning, agony-contorted Going, Noris knelt up and reached for his holstered Army Colt. With the big Texan's attention on Heaps, the soldier felt certain that he could draw and shoot undetected. Nor did Noris expect any repercussions to follow his actions. No officer in the Occupation Army would dare deal too harshly with a Federal soldier who shot down an un-Reconstructed Rebel under the prevailing conditions.

Once again Libby saw the danger to Mark, but was less suitably positioned to help him avert it. Her shotgun rested in its boot on the inside of the wagon's driving box and her Derringer was in the reticule which she had left on the store's counter when coming to see the cause of the commotion.

Swinging her gaze around the onlookers, she saw a familiar figure among them. It was a man who she believed would dare the wrath of the Union Army by intervening, even if none of the other spectators showed signs of doing so.

"Tam!" Libby shouted and saw that the man she addressed was already taking cards in the affair.

"Leave your gun where it is, soldier!"

Cold and authoritative, the words which smote Noris's ears had a Texas drawl underlaid by a Scottish burr. They also carried an implied threat that caused the soldier's head to swivel hurriedly around. What Noris saw caused him to snatch his fingers from the flap of the holster as if the leather had suddenly become red hot.

From his low-crowned grey Stetson to the soles of his high-heeled, spur-decorated boots, the speaker did not exceed five foot nine inches. He made up in hard-muscled breadth what he lacked in height, but without appearing to be heavy or clumsy. Clothed in a buckskin shirt and Mexican-styled trousers, he had a gunbelt about his waist which supported a walnut-handled Dragoon Colt tied low on his right thigh, and a Scottish dirk swung at his left hip. Neither the ·revolver nor the knife particularly interested Noris at that moment. Instead, he stared at the short, double-barreled ten-gauge shot-gun that the man was lining in his direction. Tanned, strong-looking, the man's rugged features expressed no hint of hesitation or weakness.

"What're you do—?" Noris croaked, remembering that he had seen the intruder visiting the colonel's quarters at the Army post the previous evening.

"I said leave your gun holstered," the man interrupted. "Then see to your *amigo*. This's gone far enough."

A view with which 1st Lieutenant Lebel appeared to be in complete agreement, although probably for different reasons. On his way to visit the de Brioudes, he had seen the fight and come to stop it.

"All right, that's enough," Lebel barked, thrusting his way through the crowd. "Put your gun away, cowboy!"

"When I'm sure I won't need it again," Mark replied and nodded to the noncom. "Which won't be until *after* your kicker there closes his holster."

Suddenly Lebel became uncomfortably aware that he had no real jurisdiction in the affair, except as it affected a member of the United States Army. Nor had he the means to enforce his will upon the big blond civilian. So he swung his attention to Heaps.

"On your feet, sergeant!" Lebel snapped. "Close your holster. What the hell's been happening here?"

Forcing himself upright, Heaps sullenly refastened the flap of his holster. The sergeant sensed danger for himself. One of the younger officers at the post, Lebel still knew how to protect himself with the *Manual of Field Regulations'* disciplinary powers. So Heaps knew that he must answer. He wondered how to do it in a way that would conform with the strict standing orders laid down by the post's commanding officer regarding the relationship of his men and the local civilians. A career officer, with no political or "liberal" axe to grind, the colonel had always insisted that the soldiers under his command should steer clear of friction or open clashes with the native Texans. He would, therefore, take a very serious line of action should he learn why the three enlisted men had attacked the blond giant.

"They jumped the big feller there for no reason I could see, mister," announced the man with the shotgun, before Heaps could produce any acceptable explanation. "Only they sure as hell picked on the wrong laddie for their games."

Darting an indignant scowl at the intruder, Heaps also recognized him as the colonel's visitor and left unsaid his proposed denial. Lebel looked at the civilian for a moment, then swung his gaze back to the sergeant.

"How about it, Heaps?" the lieutenant demanded, not quite sure of his ground and wanting to avoid taking chances of doing the wrong thing.

"Why don't we say it was a piece of horsing around that got a mite too rough, mister?" Mark suggested, lowering the hammer and holstering his Colt. "It'll likely be easier for all concerned that way."

"I'll go with you on that, friend," declared the man with the shotgun.

"Is that what happened, Sergeant Heaps?" Lebel insisted, not willing to appear too openly influenced by the civilians' comments.

"It was like the bee—big feller said—sir," the sergeant growled, looking slightly relieved. "We was just horsing around and it got too rough."

"Do you want to make charges against these men?" Lebel asked the big blond, indicating the three soldiers.

"Nope," Mark replied. "I'm willing to forget the whole thing, if they are."

Feelings of friendship for the soldiers did not influence Mark's attitude. The last thing he wanted was for the incident to be taken any further. If it should be, the whole of the previous night's affair would be brought into the open. So far Lansing and the other card players had kept quiet about what they had found on breaking into Mark's room. That was in part due to Ben Thompson's warning about the blond giant's probable reaction to idle gossip on the subject. In addition, the Vicomte had asked that they should not embarrass his wife by discussing the "attempted attack" upon her. While disinterested in how the truth would affect the Vicomtesse, Mark had no wish to have Libby's participation made public.

"Very well," Lebel said coldly. "If you feel that way, we'll let the matter drop. Take these men back to the post, Sergeant. I'll be seeing *you* later."

"Yo!" Heaps grunted. "Help Going up, Noris, and move out."

"My apologies for this incident," Lebel said stiffly to Mark, watching the three soldiers depart.

"It's forgotten," the big blond drawled. "Likely they didn't mean any real harm with their fooling."

Letting out a sniff that might have meant anything, the lieutenant made a smart about-face and marched off after his men. Satisfied that there would be no further developments, the crowd broke up and moved away.

"You said that as if you meant it," Libby remarked, walking toward the big blond. She looked by him and continued, "I'm real pleased to see you, Tam."

Mark turned his attention to the man whose intervention had most likely saved his life. Stepping from the sidewalk, Libby went forward with a smile and her right hand extended. Showing equal pleasure, the stocky man cradled the shotgun on the crook of his left arm.

Although his rescuer had not made any adjustments to them since taking the shotgun out of line on Private Noris, the blond giant noticed that the hammers rested at the safe half-cock position. If the man had been bluffing, it was a safe enough bluff. Nobody in his right mind would take a chance when looking into the yawning twin tubes of a ten-gauge shotgun.

"You look younger and lovelier than when I last saw you, Libby," the man answered, shaking hands with every indication of pleasure.

"And you're as big a liar," Libby smiled, clearly delighted by the compliment. "Tam, this young feller you helped's Big Rance Counter's boy, Mark. Mark, get acquainted with Tam Breda."

"Howdy, Tam," greeted Mark as the man reluctantly released Libby's hand to take his. "Say, you're Colin Farquharson's kinsman."

"Aye," agreed Breda. "I heard he was working for you, Libby."

"Yes," the blonde replied. "Colin's with us. He's engaged to marry Jeanie."

"*Bueno!*" enthused Breda. "Are they in town the now?"

"Nope. They stayed behind to move camp on to the Upper Guadalupe. We're headed out to join them as soon's we're loaded."

"I heard about Colin's run-in with the Flores bunch, Libby," Breda said, sounding a trifle defensive. "Trouble being that I was on business in Austin and he'd handed them their needings before I could come back."

"Ole Colin sure did that," Mark put in, taking a liking to the stocky man. "Hey! I didn't thank you for cutting in and helping me, Tam."

"Any friend of Libby's can count on my help every time," Breda replied, showing his relief at finding the blonde and Mark did not hold it against him that he had failed to come to his kinsman's assistance. "I'm going up to Kerrville, Libby. I'd admire to ride along with you."

"Feel free," offered Libby. "We'll be pulling out after we've ate at noon."

"Why don't you both come down to the Grand Hotel and eat with me?" Breda suggested.

"That'll suit us fine," confirmed Libby and Mark nodded his agreement.

"Say, Mark," Breda remarked. "Why did those fellers jump you? I'd reckon they was waiting for you to come out of the store."

"I couldn't say," Mark answered truthfully, for he would not lie to Breda nor explain the reason. "Just ornery, likely."

"Likely," grunted Breda. "I've a few things to tend to, so I'll see you at the Grand around noon."

"He's a nice feller," Mark commented as Breda strolled off along the sidewalk.

"Real nice," Libby agreed, then a slight flush came to her cheeks as she saw her companion's smile. "Shucks, he grew up with Trader and me back around San Antonio. Went mustanging with us a few times. Then he up and rode off to join Captain Jack Cureton's Rangers just afore the War."

"They did good work," Mark admitted.

"Tam couldn't help being away on business while Colin was facing up to the Flores boys," Libby declared.

"I didn't reckon he could," Mark assured her. "Like I said, he's a real nice feller and he'd do to ride the river with."

"Come on," Libby said hurriedly. "Let's go get the wagon loaded."

Watching the blonde return to the store, Mark grinned. If he read the signs correctly, she had not been averse to meeting Breda again and looked forward to having his company during the journey to Kerr County. Maybe she even hoped that he could extend the period of accompanying her. Not that Mark considered that to be any of his business. Libby was mature enough to know what she was doing.

For all that, Mark felt puzzled by Breda. He owed the stocky Scot his life and liked what he had seen of the other, but he could not help wondering why that bow-necked young Yankee lieutenant had so readily accepted Breda's—*a Texan's*—version of the incident and made little attempt to disprove it.

CHAPTER SIX

"Can't you-all just count on old Mark to pull the easy chores?" demanded the Ysabel Kid indignantly. "There's him a-whooping and a-womanizing down to Fort Sawyer while we're working like there's only one day left to do it."

If the Indian-dark youngster expected his comment to produce any sympathy, he was to meet with a disappointment.

"Yah!" Jeanie Schell scoffed. "You're all riled 'n' ornery 'cause you've got to do some work afoot."

"So I should be," protested the Kid. "Walking's only fitting for hosses, food-dawgs, mules, squaws 'n' white folks."

"In that order?" asked Colin Farquharson.

"All the way 'n' all the time," confirmed the Kid.

"Day's going to come when a gal'll show you a squaw's good for some things that a horse or a food-dog isn't," Dusty Fog warned. "See if it don't."[1]

"Damned if I can think what them 'things' 'd be," grinned the Kid, taking one of the coiled ropes from by the *caracol's* gate. "Well, seeing's there ain't no chance of getting out of it, let's make a start."

With the *manada de hermanos* safely in the enclosure, the mustanging party had to carry out the even more difficult and exacting task of securing them so that they could be removed. For one thing, the *caracol* had neither food nor water to supply the needs of the horses. Nor

---

[1] How Calamity Jane proved this to the Kid is told in *White Stallion, Red Mare*.

could it be used to trap other *manadas* with the young stallions running loose inside.

There were various methods by which the securing could be carried out. Some mustangers fastened a forked stick to a front ankle of each horse, the shank positioned to trip the animal by tangling its rear legs if it moved at any gait swifter than a walk. Others lashed a block of wood to the mustang's foretop which swung and banged against the horse's face when it ran. In California, the *mesteneros* frequently blindfolded their catches and allowed the wild horses to mingle with domesticated mounts. In their sightless condition, the mustangs stuck close to the other horses. Probably the most cruel method was that of the Paiute Indians, stitching shut the nostrils of their captives.

Being humane as well as a shrewd businessman, Trader Schell would have nothing to do with such cruel methods. He had taught his family that the unnecessarily brutal treatment could be avoided and defeated its own ends. Far too many of the captured horses died as a result of it. Maybe Trader Schell's ways meant more work, but his losses rarely went higher than one in twenty. That compared favorably against the one out of five which died after being caught by the crueller members of the mustanging business. Nor did the matter end there. The Schells' horses could be trained with greater facility and fewer of them became unmanageable outlaws or mind-less, nervous wrecks.

Entering the *caracol* on foot, carrying coiled ropes and other equipment, the men paired off and made ready to start work. Jeanie hovered in the background, available to help any couple requiring assistance.

Picking a brown stallion from among the milling *manada*, Dusty swung his rope and made a fast hooley-ann throw.[1] He aimed true, the loop falling over the horse's head and tightening about its neck. Feeling the touch of the hard-plaited Manila fibres, the brown reared upon its hind legs in an attempt to escape. That was the

[1] The hooley-ann throw is described fully in *Trail Boss*.

reaction sought by the small Texan.

Working as Dusty's partner, the Kid brought off a *mangana* throw. Right hand turned downward, he sent his loop flying in the horse's direction so that the circle of rope stood almost vertically. With perfect timing, the Kid's loop encircled the horse's raised and pawing forelegs. A flick of his wrists tightened the rope about them. As they returned to the ground, the trapped legs caused the horse to tumble on to its side.

Darting in as the animal tried to rise, Dusty girthed its body with a rawhide strap. While the Kid held both ropes, deftly controlling the stallion's attempts to free itself or turn on and bite Dusty, the small Texan buckled another strap to its near rear fetlock. The upper end of the strap connected to the girth and, on being drawn tight, raised the left hoof from the ground.

Having fixed the *sarprima*, as mustangers called such a device, the Texans removed their ropes. Although able to stand and move with limited freedom, the fastenings effectively prevented the stallion from traveling at any speed.

Already the more experienced *mestenero* duos had completed the application of their first *sarprimas* and moved on to the next horse they had selected for treatment. Allowing the brown to walk away, Dusty picked out and roped a washy bay. The hooley-ann head-catch fell with an equal precision to his first attempt. Ensnared by the Kid's *mangana* throw, the horse went down. However, the *sarprima* was not applied by the team.

"Hey, Jeanie-gal!" called the Kid. "Take a look at this here sorry-looking critter Dusty's catched."

Joining the speaker, the girl agreed with his opinion of the horse. Cow-hocked, long-backed and with its legs "coming out of the same hole" in its narrow chest, the horse had a very poor conformation.

"He's no use," Jeanie declared. "We couldn't even sell him to you OD Connected yahoos. Turn him loose until we're through."

The work of applying the *sarprimas* continued. Not all

the horses accepted the treatment with docility. There were several narrow escapes as members of the mustanging party had to leap or dart clear of lashing hooves and snapping teeth. Dusty came close to having to shoot one stallion, more determined than its companions to make mischief. However, Carlos's and Bernardo's ropes augmented his own and the Kid's. Between them, the four men enforced their will on the recalcitrant mustang and strapped up its leg. Being released, it attempted to carry on the dispute. It tripped and the force of the fall knocked all the aggression from it.

Roped by Colin, a coyote-dun horse refused to rear and allow Felix to use the *mangana*. Instead, it advanced and backed away with all four hooves close to the ground. Its tactics availed it nothing. Coming in from the left instead of at the front. Félix demonstrated the difference between *mangana* and a forefooting throw.

Out sailed the short, leathery-faced *mestenero's* rope. The medium-sized loop passed over the stallion's right shoulder and a little ahead of it, in a position to accept both front feet as it moved forward. Giving an inward twist to the stem of the rope, Félix made it flip to the rear and caused the loop to rise, striking against the horse's knees. A jerk on the stem completed the throw and brought the coyote-dun down. Giving it no time to recover. Félix dashed in and fastened on the *sarprima*.

About to cast a loop at a passing dark brown horse, Bernardo noticed its splayed feet, ewe-neck and signs of age. Such a decrepit-looking animal would be of no use to any buyer, so he did not waste his team's time by catching it.

At last, with the sun sinking toward the western horizon, the work was completed. Twenty-four stallions hobbled slowly in the grip of their *sarprimas* and five others were driven from the *caracol* to resume their freedom. The five had been discarded as too old or mediocre to be of use.

"Whoooee!" Jeanie breathed, watching the rejected horses racing away. "I'm not sorry that's over."

"Or me," Colin admitted, slipping an arm about her

waist and squeezing it gently. "Hey, Lon. How about you and I standing the first watch? We Scots and Indians are better able to accept hardships than the lesser peoples of the world."

"Seeing's you put it that way, I'm on," answered the Kid. "Only it's *Injuns* and *Scots*."

"Come on, Jeanie, *mesteneros*," Dusty called. "Let's get going before these pair of blasted heathens stomp up a war-dance."

Although Jeanie had hoped that Colin would ride back to the camp with her, she raised no objections. A guard would have to be set on the corral until morning. The horses could not be moved before the next day, so required watching over to protect them from human beings or prowling predatory animals. Colin always took his share of such duties, so Jeanie read no special significance in his suggestion.

"Don't you pair let anybody sneak them away from you," the girl ordered, then went to collect her horse.

"We made a good gather, Lon," Colin remarked after Jeanie, Dusty, and the *mesteneros* had gone from sight.

"Why sure," agreed the Kid. "Likely Dusty'll take most of 'em for our *remuda*. 'Les we lose too many gelding 'em, they ought to do for us."

Only geldings were permitted in a ranch's *remuda*. Stallions tended to fight and mares had the habit of bunch-quitting when on heat, taking several susceptible males along with them. So the mustangs captured that day would need to be castrated before joining the others which had been rendered acceptable for use by the OD Connected's cowhands.

"We'll not lose many," Colin promised. "Félix's better than any trained veterinarian I've seen at gelding."

"He's tolerable good," admitted the Kid. "Must've learned from the *Nemenuh*."

"Isn't there *anything* you Comanches can't do better than other people?" Colin inquired, knowing *"Nemenuh"* meant "The People" and was the Comanches' name for their tribe.

"Can't rightly think of it, even *if* there could be," the

Kid declared and eyed his companion in a speculative manner. "Did you-all have some special reason for asking me to stay on here with you?"

"I need some advice."

"Which's anybody, near on, 'd tell you, you've come to the best feller around to give it. What's up?"

"I want to catch Mogollon."

If Colin expected the Kid to show surprise, or any other emotion, he was to be disappointed. The dark youngster nodded soberly and drawled, "I figure you've got a good reason for wanting him."

"Jeanie would like to have him," Colin replied. "But there's more to it than that. The way I see it, Lon, mustanging as we're doing it in Texas right now can't go on for too many years."

"How'd you make that out, *amigo*?" asked the Kid. "There're plenty of wild hosses around."

"That there are, right now. But not for much longer. Not good horses, anyway. You saw what happened today. After we'd caught the *manada*, we turned five of them loose again."

"They weren't worth keeping," the Kid pointed out.

"That's what I mean," Colin elaborated. "Ever since Texans and Mexicans started catching mustangs, they've turned the worthless animals back on to the range. They've caught or killed the *manaderos* and the culls are given chances to mate with mares that wouldn't come with healthy stallions around. So the culls pass their faults on to the foals. The stock gets poorer. In twenty years, the mustangs will hardly be worth the trouble of catching."

"Maybe not even in that long," the Kid said.

Colin had expressed a sentiment which Dusty, Mark and the Kid had discussed several times. All of them knew enough about breeding and bloodlines to figure that the continued removal of quality animals and return of culls must eventually ruin the conformation, stamina and speed of the wild horses roaming the range country. Under natural conditions, only the hardiest, best-qualified stallions had the opportunity to stamp their characteristics on the breed. With them gone, the mediocre males could breed and lay their fault-filled mark upon the future generations.

"I don't aim to wait until it happens," Colin continued. "It's something I've talked over with Libby and Jeanie. We're going to get some land, maybe around here, settle down and raise a fine strain of horses. Mogollon strikes me as being a good start to it."

"He'll be that all right. Only ole Mogollon's not going to be took easy."

"Do you say it can't be done?"

"You know as well as I do that taking a *manadero's* near on impossible."

"You did it with your Nigger horse," Colin said.

"He wasn't no *manadero* when pappy 'n' me caught him," the Kid objected. "And he was a whole heap younger'n Mogollon. From all I've heard, that big stallion's fast, smart 'n' tolerable mean. Could be he'll turn out like that black cuss today, too mean to be took alive."

"He was captured once."

"Why sure—and got away again."

"Could we get him?" Colin insisted.

"You're fixing to try, no matter what I say," the Kid guessed. "So's soon's we're relieved and I've fed, I'll take my ole Nigger hoss and go look for him." He slapped a hand against his thigh and grinned, "Hey! I didn't know you Scotch fellers did it."

"Did what?"

"Went out 'n' got a real good hoss to give to your gal's kinfolk. Us Comanches do it a mite different, though. We have to hand over the hoss afore the gal's been asked, said 'yes' 'n' nailed our hides to the lodge pole."

"How do we go about it?" Colin inquired, ignoring the comment.

"Was I you," answered the Kid, "I'd talk some to Jeanie about that."

"It's to be a surprise," Colin protested.

"And she'll act like it is when you tell her," grinned the Kid. "Then she'll set to and help you-all every which-way she can."

"You think I couldn't do it without the lassie's help?"

"Put your tail down and stop them horns a-hooking, *amigo*. You'll need that *mestenera's* help. And, believe me, that's more damned help 'n' hoss-savvy than you could get from anybody else."

"More than from a *Nemenuh*?" Colin challenged, his good humor restored.

"If saying so'll get you to ask her," drawled the Kid, "even from a *Nemenuh*."

Having asked for advice, Colin showed sufficient good sense to accept it. On his return to the camp, he took Jeanie to one side and stated his intentions. She immediately threw herself wholeheartedly into helping him and agreed to the Kid departing to locate Mogollon's *manada*.

Leaving after supper, the Kid returned while the rest of the party were eating breakfast. Taking no notice of the manner in which Colin and Jeanie looked at him, he collected his food. Squatting on his heels, he finished the meal without saying a word. Not until he had dropped his plate and tin cup into the dish of hot water by the chuckwagon did he offer to address the impatient girl and Scot.

"*Ka-dih's* sure favouring you, Scotch brother."

"Scottish," Colin corrected almost automatically. "'Scotch' is a drink."

"You can buy the white part of me one next time we're in town," suggested the Kid. "I've never seed a feller so lucky."

"How come?" demanded Jeanie.

"Did I ever tell you about me 'n' Grandpappy Long Walker on our first bear hunt, Dusty?" the Kid inquired.

"Did *I* mention to *you* how we ought to get somebody out with a shovel to bury that black *manadero*, Dusty?" Jeanie asked, staring pointedly at the Kid. "I'd say it's a chore for one of your OD Connected hands."

"Us bosses all stick together, Lon," Dusty warned, having been an amused onlooker to that point. "And riding the blister end of a shovel's hard work."

"How'd you know?" the Kid said truculently. "I've

never seed a boss riding one. All right. Peace, white sister." The last words, being accompanied by the traditional sign of peace, came with great solemnity as Jeanie moved threateningly toward him. "I know when I'm licked."

"I never figured you knowed nothing," Jeanie sniffed.

"I know ole Mogollon's back down this ways," stated the Kid. "Fact being, him 'n' his *manada*'re heading for the place where we picked up the last bunch."

"Unless it's been tried since last year," Jeanie put in, eyes dancing with eagerness, "the *Caracol de Santa Bárbara's* one pen nobody's tried to run him into. Colin, this could be our chance."

Once a *manada* had thwarted an attempt to force them into a *caracol*, it was impossible to drive them into that location again. So, if Mogollon's band had not been pushed toward the *Caracol de Santa Bárbara*, Jeanie and her men might capture the stallion. They had already made a successful *corrida* and so possessed a knowledge of the type of ground they must cover.

"Best get started at it then," Dusty said.

"Sure," Jeanie agreed. "Fernan, take a wagon team and haul that *manadero's* body a mile or so away from the valley. Félix, take the boys and drive those hosses we caught yesterday up here."

"*Si, mestenera,*" the segundo replied. "Saddle up *amigos.*"

Normally the newly captured horses would have been left in the *caracol* for a few days, to let them settle down and adjust to captivity. With the chance to collect Mogollon, Jeanie and her men changed the procedure. Going to the pen, they drove the mustangs, still held by the *sarprimas*, out of the draw and moved them back to the camp area. During the journey, such of the mustangs as had not already made the discovery learned that they could not run with one leg raised from the ground. After falling once, the horses gave up their attempts at flight.

In the middle of the afternoon, Colin sat with Jeanie and Dusty among the post oaks. The rest of the men were in the positions they had used to take part in the *corrida* for the *manada de hermanos*. There had been only one alteration to the arrangements. Knowing how important the capture of Mogollon was to Colin and Jeanie, the Kid had taken the girl's place in the valley.

Excitement and anticipation showed on the girl's face as she sat her *tobiano* gelding between the two men. Listening to the skirl of Colin's bagpipes, Jeanie and Dusty studied Mogollon's reaction to the sound. Like other horses hearing the pipes for the first time, the *manadero* could not decide whether the strange noise was a menace to its band. Adopting the safe course, Mogollon began to move its family away from the unnatural wailing.

"Let's go and get them!" Jeanie hissed and started her black and white mount moving.

On seeing the riders, Mogollon gave a snort of warning. Obediently, the rest of the *manada* started to run. Satisfied that everything was going as they had planned, the girl and her companions let out wild yells and gave chase. With their horses moving at a gallop, the trio spread out to a wide arrowhead formation. Filled with eagerness, Jeanie once again drew slightly ahead.

Throwing a look behind, Mogollon increased its speed. Passing down the flank of the *manada*, the chestnut stallion forced the leaders to turn. Instead of fleeing into the valley where the Kid and the *mesteneros* were waiting to head them toward the *caracol*, the band reversed their course so as to pass at an angle ahead of their three pursuers.

Nearest of the trio, Colin urged his horse on at a greater speed in the hope of cutting off the mustangs. Coming ahead of its harem as if they had been standing still, Mogollon rushed at the Scot. Faced by the teeth-flashing fury of the *manadero*, Colin's blue-roan mount showed an equal aversion to that displayed by Dusty's *bayo-cebrunos* when charged by the black master-stallion.

Rearing high on its hind legs, the blue-roan pivoted around. Taken by surprise, Colin slid backwards from his insecure perch and tumbled to the ground. Seeing her fiancé unhorsed, Jeanie came the closest in her lifetime to acting from blind panic. She slammed her spur-decorated heels against the *tobiano's* ribs. Responding to the signal, it thrust itself forward at an increased pace. In doing so, it came between Dusty and Colin. Although he had already drawn his right-side Colt, Dusty dare not shoot for fear of hitting the girl.

Looking past Jeanie, Dusty saw Colin throw himself on to his back and roll face down. Even as the Scot covered his head with his arms, Mogollon hurdled his body without breaking stride. All around Colin, the hooves of the *manada* thudded and pounded on the ground. Only the horses' natural aversion to treading on alien objects saved him. One colt's near fore hoof crushed the eagle's feather in his bonnet as it lay just in front of his head. Unable to swerve in time, a female foal bounded over his broad back and brushed against him in passing. Then the whole band had gone by, streaming across the range, with Mogollon resuming its position at the rear. Holstering his Colt, Dusty made no attempt to follow them.

Leaving her *tobiano's* back almost at a full gallop, Jeanie lit down to run and kneel by Colin's side. He forced himself on to his hands and knees, staring in disappointment after the departing horses.

"Are you hurt, honey?" Jeanie gasped.

"Only my pride, lassie," Colin answered, turning his gaze from the *manada* to her anxious features. "What happened?"

"That tricky son-of-a-bitch!" Jeanie spluttered, directing a furious glare in Mogollon's direction. "He knew what we was at and wouldn't let us drive him. I bet he'll turn back every time he gets chased. Damn it! He's too all-fired smart to let his-self get hazed into a *caracol*."

CHAPTER SEVEN

About to enter the Grand Hotel accompanied by Mark Counter, Libby Schell saw Tam Breda strolling over from the rear of the building. The loading of her wagon had been completed without further interruptions and Libby was looking forward to a pleasant journey to Kerr County. Her smile wavered as Breda darted a glance into the barroom and swung to face it. As he strode toward the door, his right hand dipped to loosen the Dragoon Colt in its holster.

"I never thought Tam'd need a drink before he could face me," Libby sniffed.

"He's expecting trouble," Mark replied, having seen the movements of the Scot's right hand. "I'd best go back his play if he needs it."

Backed up against the mahogany bar, a tall, slim young man with a swarthy, Gallic cast of features and wearing cheap town clothes, looked about him in bewilderment. Before him, exuding menace, stood a tall, slender, handsome, professional gambler. Off to one side, a pair of hard-faced men in range clothes glowered at him and kept their right hands thumb-hooked close to their holstered revolvers. At the other side, farther away and to the rear of the men, a beautiful brunette watched with a dispassionate gaze. While she did not wear the garish, abbreviated dress of a saloon worker, nobody would have mistaken her for a "good" woman.

"Damned if I know what to make of it," declared the gambler in ringing tones. "I go out of here for five minutes and when I come back, here's this jasper a-pawing at my wife."

"M'sieur!" gasped the man at the bar. "I wasn't. I was sh—he—your wife—"

"You hear that, gents?" demanded the gambler, addressing the words to the hard-cases, the worried looking bartender and a skinny, sly-featured man who sat at a table in the left hand corner of the room. "This here foreign son-of-a-bitch's laying the blame on my Laura-gal."

"Such doings should oughta be stopped, stranger," stated the taller of the hovering hard-cases.

"They sure as hell should," agreed his companion. "Go get me a bottle of whiskey, barkeep."

"Sure," replied the bartender. "Look, fellers—"

"Do I have to come over and fetch it myself?" growled the second hard-case.

"N—No," answered the bartender. "Only I don't want—"

Seeing the ugly expression on the hard-case's surly features, the bartender turned away. Instantly the first hard-case reached behind his back to the Colt revolver thrust into his waist-band and concealed beneath his calfskin vest. Drawing the weapon, he tossed it at the frightened Gallic man. In an involuntary gesture, the man caught the revolver.

"Watch him, Hubie!" screeched Laura. "He's pulled a gun on you!"

Across flashed the gambler's right hand, passing under the left flap of his coat. Even as his fingers closed on the butt of the Colt Wells Fargo revolver hidden there, something crashed against his right shoulder blade with numbing force. Letting out a cry of pain, he stumbled forward and his hand fell limply to his side.

Startled exclamations burst from Laura—whose language proved that she was not "good"—and the two hard-cases as they saw a whiskey bottle flash by them and strike the gambler's back. Snarling curses, the pair began to turn and reach for their guns. What they saw ended their movements in that direction.

Entering the room unnoticed by its occupants, Tam Breda had realized the significance of what he saw. On a table to the right of the entrance was a tray holding bottles and glasses from the poker game that had resumed upstairs. Snatching up a bottle, he had hurled it with all his strength. That had been the only way, other than using a bullet, he could think of to prevent Hubie Stagge from killing the scared man at the bar. From flinging the bottle, Breda's right hand dipped to produce his Dragoon Colt. By the time Royce and Coxin, Stagge's confederates, had recovered from their surprise and started to turn, Breda's gun was already lined at them.

Colliding with the bar alongside his staring, frightened would-be victim, Stagge twisted around. His left hand went up to massage the throbbing shoulder and his eyes flamed hatred which he hoped would hold the advancing Breda's attention. Although Coxin and Royce could not take cards, there were other factors unsuspected by the Scot in the game. Dipping her right hand into the reticule which swung from her left wrist, Laura moved soft-footed to get behind Breda. Also to his rear, the man in the corner started to rise and draw a Colt.

Just as Stagge was congratulating himself on having an old enemy in a box, he saw a huge, blond cowhand and a buxom blonde woman come into the room. With a fresh flood of anger, the gambler realized that the trap might not be sprung upon Breda.

Seeing the man in the corner, Mark turned, drew his right hand Colt and yelled, "Drop it, *hombre*!"

The man might look sly and shifty, but he possessed good, sound common sense. Knowing that such flashing speed was mostly accompanied by considerable accuracy, he rapidly placed his revolver on the table and shot both hands into the air.

Bringing a derringer from her reticule, Laura prepared to avenge her "husband's" injury. Although she heard the patter of footsteps behind her, she ignored them—at first. A hand gripped Laura's shoulder and swung her around. On turning, she had a brief impression of an angry, good-looking female face and blonde hair. From the corner of her eye, Laura caught just a glimpse of a fist growing in size as it hurled in her direction. The hard knuckles crashed against the side of her jaw. Exploding patches of brilliant light obscured the brunette's vision. Vaguely she felt herself spin around, then everything went black. Taking Libby's power-packed punch so unexpectedly, the brunette was propelled sideways. Striking a table, she rolled across its top and flopped in a flaccid manner to the floor.

"If that bit—woman's hurt Laura—!" Stagge blazed, not particularly caring but feeling he should make the comment.

"She'll've got no more than she asked for," Breda answered, glancing to where Libby was picking up Laura's discarded Derringer. Then he looked at the gambler and continued, "You should try a new game, Stagge. That one's getting known."

"What's it about, Tam?" Mark inquired, watching the skinny man.

"Mr. Stagge here's a hired butcher, laddie," Breda explained.

"That's never been proved!" Stagge spat out.

"No," Breda agreed. "He does it all nice and legal. Every man he's dropped's had a gun in his hand. Like this young feller would have had if I hadn't cut in. You'd best give me the gun, friend."

"Wha—?" gasped the proposed victim. "I—Here, take it, *m'sieur*."

"Who hired you to kill him, Stagge, and why?" demanded Breda, accepting the revolver thrust in his direction.

"I don't know what you mean," the gambler snarled. "He was a-pawing Laura—"

"Was it that way 'round," Libby commented dryly, "I'd say she's been pawed plenty. And done some pawing herself."

"Yeah?" Stagge snarled at the blonde. "And I've heard—"

"Just what did you hear, *hombre*?" Mark asked, his Colt turning toward the speaker's belly.

"Nothing!" Stagge muttered.

Although Stagge had not heard about the previous night's incident, he held back his intended accusation. There was an air of menace about the blonde giant and the Colt lined with disconcerting accuracy. So Stagge did not repeat the vicious fabrication about Libby's amatory relationship with her Mexican *mesteneros* since Trader Schell's death.

Before the affair could be taken further, Sheriff Lansing and other people arrived. To Mark, it seemed that the local peace officer looked to Tam Breda for guidance and went willingly along with the Scot's suggestions that the gambler and other participants be taken to the jail for questioning. Mark felt puzzled. A political appointee, Lansing had never been an efficient sheriff. Yet Mark could not understand why he allowed Breda to give him even the correct advice.

"I'm sorry, Libby lass," Breda said. "I'll have to go tend to this afore I leave town. I'll come back as quickly as I can."

Watching the party leave, with Stagge supporting a wobbly legged Laura, Libby frowned. Tam Breda was behaving like a peace officer, but that could not be. One of the first acts performed by the Reconstruction administration had been to disband the Ranger companies. So Tam—*her* Tam, as she now regarded him—could no longer be wearing a badge. If he should be—Libby did not want to consider that possibility. Still frowning, she accompanied Mark to the dining room.

Half an hour went by before Breda joined them and apologized for his absence. During that time, they had not mentioned him except in general terms. To Mark, it had seemed that Libby had wanted to avoid discussing the incident's implications.

"What happened down to the sheriff's office, Tam?" Mark inquired.

"Not much," Breda answered disgustedly. "Stagge and his bunch stuck to their story about the man accosting Laura. The barkeep hadn't been there when she started 'ticing the feller. That skinny-gutted cuss's one of 'em and he goes along with the tale. Trouble being, I can't prove he's in cahoots with Stagge."

"He was trying to pull down on you," Libby pointed out.

"And allows he aimed to help me," Breda replied. "The only way we could've proved different would've been after he'd shot me."

"I'm sorry I billed in and spoiled it for you," Mark said with a grin.

"I'm not!" Breda declared. "So it's that feller's word against the boiling of 'em. Sure, I know what they aimed to do. But I can't take 'em in front of a judge and prove it."

"What set them on to that feller?" Libby inquired, rather than ask why an ex-Texas Ranger should want to take Stagge's bunch into court.

"They wouldn't say and he couldn't even start to guess," Breda answered. "There doesn't seem to be any reason why anybody'd want him dead bad enough to pay Stagge for doing it. He's just a cook, headed west looking for work. That was why he went to the Grand; got told at the stage depot that they might be hiring."

"He talked sort of French," Mark commented. "There's a French count and his missus at the hotel—"

"I thought some on that," admitted Breda. "Trouble being, the feller's a Creole from down Louisiana way and's never been to France. Anyways, let's forget it. The feller's not got work and's heading west on the stage this afternoon. Lansing's holding Stagge's bunch until after he's gone. There's nothing I can do. It's not in my bailiwick."

"Shouldn't be, seeing's you're not with the Rangers no more," Libby remarked, the words coming despite her desire to avoid hearing an explanation.

"Nope," Breda said, looking uncomfortable. "I'm a captain in the State Police now, Libby."

Going by Libby's intake of breath, Mark concluded that the news of Breda's new employment did not meet with her approval. He could guess why.

Brought in to replace the Texas Rangers, Governor Davis's State Police had rapidly made themselves hated.

Many of its officers were vicious, corrupt opportunists eager to line their pockets at the Texans' expense; or "liberals" seeking to work their bigoted hatred against the supporters of the Confederate States. The enlisted men were of the same kind, with a number of the worst type of white-hating Negroes to swell their ranks.

Loyal to the Southern cause, for family rather than political reasons, Libby had accepted Breda's reasons for not joining the Confederate States' Army. Like her husband, he had carried out an important task at home. Trader had supplied remounts to the Rebel cavalry or artillery. Riding with Cureton's Rangers, Breda had helped to protect the homes of men—regardless of whether they wore blue or grey—away fighting the War. To learn that Breda had accepted an important rank in the State Police drove a chill of anger through her. One of that force's victims had been her brother, killed while "resisting arrest" by an officer who wanted to take over his property.

Jerking her head around, without giving Breda the opportunity to explain his "treachery," Libby started to talk pointedly to Mark. The remainder of the meal was not a success, due to her behavior. Glancing at Breda, Mark could see his lips tighten and tried to lessen the tension. Libby showed no sign of repenting, but the Scot accompanied her and Mark to the wagon. One the way, Mark felt annoyed and embarrassed by the way Libby was acting toward him. Sure they had made love the previous night, but he had expected that the dawn would see the incident over. In her annoyance at Breda, Libby seemed likely to make a fool of herself.

The situation did not improve during the journey out of town. After Mark and Breda had collected their horses, they set off with Libby's party. By the time they had set up camp for the night, the big blond had decided that she must be taught a lesson and brought back to her senses. Just as he hoped, she played into his hands. They had made camp in a clearing a short distance from the Kerrville trail. Surrounded by trees and bushes, the area's water supply was about a hundred yards away. With the fire built, Libby asked Mark to help her collect water.

"Sure," the big blond agreed, picking up a couple of buckets and conscious of Breda watching the by-play. "I'd admire to, Libby."

Neither of them spoke as they passed out of sight from the camp. On reaching the edge of a small stream, Mark set down the buckets. Turning, he scooped Libby into his arms and lowered his head as if to kiss her. In bed the previous night, she had responded with passionate eagerness. Instead of repeating her reactions, he felt her body stiffen violently and strain back. Surprise and anger showed on her face as she twisted her head away.

"Let me go!" Libby hissed furiously. "What the hell do you think I am?"

Immediately, grinning broadly, Mark lifted her gently back to arms' length. Setting her on her feet, he took his hands away and watched her clench her fists.

"Until noon today, I'd've said a real nice lady and a right smart woman."

"Only what?" Libby challenged, drawing back her right fist a little.

"Now I'm starting to wonder."

"Because I slept with you?"

"That ended well afore noon and did nothing to change my thoughts about you," Mark drawled. "It was pleasurable, only I don't figure you'd do it regular—or even again with me."

"Then why—?" Libby gasped, letting her hands drop to her sides.

"To prove it for certain to both of us," Mark explained, picking up the buckets. "And to try to stop you doing something real foolish."

"How do you mean?"

"With Tam Breda. Keep on acting like you've been doing since you learned about him joining the State Police and you're likely to run him off for good."

"Is that any of your never-mind?" demanded Libby.

"Maybe not," admitted Mark. "'Cepting I like you and Tam both. Did you figure to ask him why he joined, or just aim to keep acting mean 'n' ornery 'cause he did it?"

"Do you know why I'm acting this way?"

"'Cause you reckon Tam helped gun down your brother."

"The hell I do!" Libby protested, so vigorously that Mark's grin grew broader. "I know he wasn't mixed up in that. Say, did Tam tell you why he joined while you was going for the horses?"

"Yes," Mark replied. "Only I'm not going to tell you."

"Will you go and ask him to come down here to me?"

"No, ma'am," Mark refused. "You're going to have to eat crow and ask him to come yourself."

"Damned if you're not a meaner cuss than I figured," Libby smiled. "Come on, I'll eat that crow."

Despite the conversation, Libby showed no sign of carrying out her promise on their return to the camp. However, she gave Breda the pick of the food and paid attention to him. Telling Mark and a *mestenero* that they had volunteered to wash the dishes, she slapped a hand to the pockets of the Levi's pants she had donned for the journey.

"Damn it!" Libby ejaculated. "I left my handkerchief by the stream. How's about coming with me to fetch it, Tam?"

"That I will, lassie," Breda agreed.

"Why did you join Davis's bunch, Tam?" Libby asked as they walked through the woods side by side. Her right hand found and gripped his left.

"He needed a man to run the law in Kerr County."

"Why you? You know what kind the State Police are."

"You've just answered your own question. Don't you reckon it'll be easier for folks with somebody like me running things—and picking fellers for the Ranger companies's'll be needed after Davis and his bunch've been run out of office?"

"It would!" Libby enthused. "If you wasn't there, some lousy soft-shell or pocket-lining carpetbagger would be. I've been acting *loco* all day, Tam."

"I've always loved you, Libby lass," Breda declared, taking her arm and turning her to face him. "I know it's not long since Trader died, but I was thinking—"

"Tam!" Libby put in, her voice strained and eyes blinking worriedly. "I slept with Mark last night."

Before she returned Breda's declaration of affection, or allowed him to go further, she wanted to be honest with him. Searching the tanned, rugged features, she could detect no condemnation or revulsion at her confession.

"You'd not've done it while Trader was alive. Nor if we'd met and I'd declared myself to you yesterday. And, not a week back, I slept with April Hosman up in San Antone."

Libby stared without speaking for several seconds. Another potential victim of the Flores brothers' vengeance, saloongirl April Hosman had remained in the Schell family's care until the deaths of the *bandidos*. During that time, she and Libby had become good friends. Once able to leave in safety, April had stated that the outdoor life was not for her. Returning first to Fort Sawyer, she had gone on to find employment in San Antonio.

"Did you enjoy it?" Libby asked at last.

"Will you be riled if I say 'yes'?" grinned Breda.

"I don't know what I'll be," Libby admitted. "But I for sure know what I'll do if it ever happens again."

With that, Libby twisted free. Walking a short way, she came to a spot where the bank of the stream rose a few feet above the water. As Libby sat down with her legs dangling over, Breda joined her and slipped his arm around her waist.

"April and me had supper," the Scot said. "Talked some about Jeanie, Colin, what's been happening. That's how I knew where to find you and headed down this way to do it. We talked some about you, too. A whole heap about you, I reckon. Next morning April said a kind of strange thing."

"What was that?" Libby inquired.

"She said she'd been wondering all night if it'd been her or you I was with," Breda answered and his left arm connected with the right behind her neck. "I know which I'd sooner it'd been."

"Which?"

"Was we engaged to be married, I'd show you."

"You can buy me the ring later," Libby breathed and allowed herself to be lowered on to her back. "Only I'm from Missouri. I've got to be shown."

CHAPTER EIGHT

Standing at the mouth of a draw, Colin studied the range ahead of him with the aid of Dusty's field glasses. Scattered in concealment in front of him, half a dozen *mesteneros* waited for the signal to commence a *corrida*. Out beyond the *mesteneros*, Mogollon's lathered and leg-weary *manada* moved uneasily. In between snatching up mouthfuls of grass, the mustangs threw nervous glances about them. Only the big chestnut stallion retained any semblance of its former alertness. Examining the *manadero*, Colin concluded that its capture was still anything but certain despite the events of the past four days.

A gloomy band of mustangers had returned to the camp after the first abortive attempt to capture Mogollon. About the only good thing any of them could say had been that at least the *manadero* was not kill-crazy. If it had been, Colin would not be alive.

There had been many methods by which the stallion might be caught discussed that night. In times of a water shortage, hanging "scarers," pieces of rag fixed to flap and blow in the breeze, at all but one of the remaining drinking holes would frighten the *manada* and bring it to the waiting *mesteneros*. There had been too much rain for that to work. Félix had told of capturing one of a band, fastening a dummy rider on its back and turning it loose. When its companions saw it coming, they would run away. It followed them until all were exhausted, at which point the *mesteneros* moved in. Unfortunately none of Mogollon's band could out-run the *manadero*. An old

Comanche Indian trick had been to turn loose a stallion near the *mestena* and catch the *manadero* as it fought with the potential rival. Jeanie had warned that, when tried on Mogollon, it had run until clear of the men, turned and killed the other stallion. Neither Jeanie nor Colin would allow the Kid to try to "crease" Mogollon. While a bullet raking across the spinal nerve would knock a horse unconscious for long enough to let it be secured, the margin for error was so slight that more animals were killed than taken by the method.

At last it had been decided that they would try to "walk down" Mogollon's band. To do that, riders working in relays followed the *manada* day and night, giving the mustangs no rest nor time to drink and graze. A *manada* always traveled in a circular route on its home range. By keeping to the inside of the circle, the men doing the "walking" covered a shorter distance than the mustangs and at a more even pace. Their horses also received adequate rest, food and water, so kept in better condition than the *manada*.

For four days, Colin, the Kid, Bernardo and Carlos had taken turns to keep after Mogollon's band. It had been hard, exacting work, but at last the time had come when they would make the final effort at catching the *manadero*.

"It's lucky that Libby and Mark got back with the rest of the men," Dusty remarked from his place at Colin's right side. "We can use their help."

"That's the living truth," agreed the Kid to Dusty's right. "Damned if ole Mogollon don't look like he could take another four days' 'walking down.'"

"There's Jeanie's signal now!" Colin put in as a sparkle of flashing light showed at the far side of the range.

"We'd better get to our horses," Dusty suggested. "Bernie and the boys'll be making their move soon."

Each of the trio had his best horse waiting with a double-girthed saddle and a new rope on the horn. Running to the animals, Dusty, the Kid and Colin gathered up the trailing reins, then mounted. Even as they were riding to the mouth of the draw, they heard

Bernardo cut loose with a ringing whoop.

Leaving their hiding places, the six *mesteneros* charged toward the *manada*. Yelling like drunken savages, they held their ropes ready to be thrown. The tired mustangs fled from the new menace, with Mogollon bringing up the rear and urging the slower animals to greater efforts. Bernardo's party did not attempt to close in on the mustangs at first, but acted as if trying to drive them toward the hill where Jeanie, Mark and Félix were waiting.

"It's working, Dusty!" Colin ejaculated. "There he goes now!"

Following the tactics it had used on the first *corrida*, Mogollon tore to the front of the *manada*. On reaching the leading mare, the *manadero* started to force her around. As if realizing that its tired band could not hope to escape in a bunch, Mogollon made a rearing, skidding, hoof-flailing turn. It gave a piercing, screaming whistle that caused the other mustangs to scatter.

Horses fled in all directions, while Bernardo and his men swept in to take what captures they could. Everything seemed to be in a state of chaos and confusion but the *mesteneros'* mounts were still fresh and not tired by a long period of continuous harrying.

Racing back the way it had come during the brief chase, Mogollon burst out of the wild mill. Always before the refusal to be driven had brought it safety. Following their orders, the *mesteneros* allowed the *manadero* to go, concentrating on the rest of the band. Each man had three ropes and hoped to make a catch on all of them. Striding out at a pace not much slower than at the start of the "walking down," the chestnut stallion approached the draw which hid Dusty, the Kid and Colin.

"Now!" Dusty hissed, freeing his rope and shaking out the loop.

Made excited by the commotion, the three big horses responded eagerly to the heel-signals of their riders. Bursting from their place of concealment like pigeons leaving a shooting-trap, Dusty's paint, the Kid's white and Colin's *bayo-lobo* spread out like the triple prongs of a fan. Like the *mesteneros'* mounts, the three big horses had done little work that day. Encouraged by their riders, they sped to cut off Mogollon's escape.

Traveling at a racing gallop, Mogollon became aware of the new danger—but just too late. At the sight of Colin bearing down on it, the stallion swerved in the wrong direction. Its new route took it across Dusty's and the Kid's front. By that time, they had reached a distance from which they could throw their ropes.

Standing up in his stirrups, Dusty swung the rope before him and up to the left. Three times he whirled it above his head, delicately testing the momentum it built up in his hand. Satisfied, he twirled the loop forward so that it passed over his right shoulder. Out sailed the Manila rope, converging with Mogollon as the *manadero* ran at an angle in front of him.

To Colin, it seemed that the loop took hours in its flight. At last it dipped down, passing around the stallion's head. A touch of Dusty's heels augmented the manipulation of the reins in his left hand. With its master still standing in the stirrups, the paint tucked its hind legs under its body and spiked its fore feet into the ground. Settling his rump on the saddle, Dusty thrust his feet forward and torso to the rear. Drawn tight between the paint, as it came to a classic sliding stop, and the running *manadero*, the loop closed around Mogollon's neck.

Brought to an abrupt halt, but not thrown down, Mogollon screamed in fury. Before the *manadero* could turn and charge at its captor, the Kid's overhead loop flew out. Instead of reining in his white as he made his catch, the youngster kept moving. Going past Mogollon, he brought his horse to a stop on the opposite side to Dusty. Their two ropes, lashed to the saddlehorns, held the master-stallion so that it could not reach either of them. Snorting, rearing and plunging, Mogollon fought against the constriction of the twin loops.

"Keep out of it unless one of us busts his rope, Colin!" Dusty yelled, controlling his paint so that it held the rope taut. "Leave us choke him down, then you do the rest."

That had been the agreement reached while they were

planning the final stage of the "walking down." All the rough handling was, if possible, to be carried out by the Texans or *mesteneros* so that Colin could treat the *manadero* with nothing but kindness. In that way, he would more easily gain Mogollon's confidence.

By keeping their big stallions backing away from the *manadero*, Dusty and the Kid cut off its air supply. Forcing themselves to ignore the hideous sound of the chestnut fighting to breathe, they choked it unconscious. When it went down, Dusty took a set of hobbles which had been tied to his cantle. Allowing his reins to fall free, he dismounted. Trained for such work, the paint kept the rope as tight as if it still carried a rider. Swiftly Dusty buckled the cuffs of the hobbles above the pastern joints on Mogollon's fore legs. With that done, he caught the hackamore thrown to him by the Kid.

Looking like a cross between a halter and a bridle, the hackamore offered all the advantages of both. It could be equipped with reins or a lead-rope, but made use of a *bosal*—a rawhide ring about the horse's head above the mouth—instead of a metal bit. In addition, there was a three-inch wide browband fitted so that it could be slid down to cover its wearer's eyes. Although he adjusted the hackamore to Mogollon's head, Dusty did not use the browband as a blindfold.

"Come on over and set him loose, Colin," Dusty said.

Leaving his horse ground-hitched, Colin walked across to the stallion. By the time he arrived, Dusty had returned to the paint. At their masters' commands, the two horses allowed the ropes to sag loosely. Colin opened and removed the loops. With the hobbles fitted, Mogollon could not travel faster than at a walk and, after being choked down, would be in no condition to make an escape bid on its recovery.

Kneeling by the stallion as it dragged air into its lungs, Colin raised its sleek head. He lowered his face to Mogollon's and blew repeatedly into the flaring nostrils. While uncertain just why it should be, he knew that doing so tended to quiet down the animal so treated. After some seconds, Mogollon regained consciousness and came, snorting and lathered, to its feet. Keeping a gentle hold on the reins, Colin spoke soothingly to the stallion. His free hand caressed its head and neck, occasionally covering the nostrils so that it would become used to his scent.

Oblivious of what was going on around her, Jeanie galloped up on her *tobiano* gelding. She went by the *mesteneros* as they swarmed around and held together the leg-weary remains of the *manada* making for what, to her, was the most important area. For all her delight, she did not attempt to ride straight up to her fiancé and the captured *manadero*. Instead, she halted alongside Dusty and the Kid.

"It was just like you figured, Dusty!" the girl enthused. "He bust back through the line."

"He tried it once too often," drawled the Kid.

Looking at Colin and Mogollon, Jeanie nodded her agreement. She realized just how much the capture of the *manadero* had been due to Dusty's grasp of the situation and tactical training. While they had all remembered the manner in which Mogollon had defeated their first *corrida*, only the small Texan had seen how it might be turned to their advantage.

Jeanie and the *mesteneros* had been all for the usual method of surrounding the exhausted mustangs, then dashing in and roping any which looked like escaping. Fortunately they had listened to Dusty's alternative suggestion. It had been at his instigation that Colin's party took up their position to the rear of the main body. Finding itself apparently being driven into danger, Mogollon had used the tactics which had saved the *manada* from capture on numerous occasions. So the trick that had previously saved Mogollon finally brought about its capture.

"*Gracias*, Dusty," Jeanie said sincerely. "You called the play just right."

"You'd likely've taken him anyways," Dusty answered.

"Maybe," the girl replied. "He was going faster'n a Nueces steer when he cut around the boys."

"Mark and Félix had to go some to catch them two young stallions," the Kid went on, nodding to where the two men were returning leading their captives. "Ole Mogollon could easy've got away."

"Talking about getting away," Dusty put in, wanting the subject changed. "I'd say it's time we thought about doing just that."

"Sure is," confirmed Jeanie and looked around. "Let's go, *mesteneros*."

Taking turns at holding the exhausted mustangs, the excited and delighted Mexicans had been riding over to study the legendary Mogollon. Wishing to avoid disturbing the stallion, none had gone close. Mogollon stood quietly, allowing Colin to wipe the lather from its flanks. When all the men had looked and commented, he turned to the Kid.

"Shall we get going, Lon?"

"Might's well," the Kid replied. "Happen we stick around here, somebody'll find *me* some work to do."

"Let us pull out first, Colin," Dusty suggested.

"Go to it," confirmed the Scot. "Only let me cover Mogollon's eyes first. If I don't, he'll raise a fuss when he sees you taking his *manada*."

Acting with calm deliberation, Colin drew the browband over the stallion's eyes. At first it snorted and moved restlessly, but its hobbled feet prevented any violent resistance. Being unable to see them go, it stood quietly as Jeanie's party drove its band away. Nor did it fight against the gentle pull of the reins as Colin led it to his waiting mount. Swinging into the saddle, he set both horses moving at a slow walk. The pace was leisurely because of the hobbles on Mogollon's legs and through the need to let the horse cool down after its exertions. Mounting his white stallion, the Kid followed Colin from a distance and in silence.

Instead of going with the others, Colin and the Kid made their way to a small corral in a valley about a mile from the main camp. The enclosure had been erected by the *mesteneros* to be used if they caught Mogollon. Flowing under one side of the corral, a small stream provided an adequate water supply and the ankle-deep grama grass offered sufficient bulk grazing during Mogollon's incarceration. Making a curve at that point, the shape of the valley and height of its sides effectively hid the surrounding country from view. The site of the corral had been selected to help persuade the *manadero* to accept Colin as its companion and master.

Gregarious by nature, a horse needed to have company. Deprived of its own kind, it would always seek to have other animals around it. So Mogollon had been brought to the valley. Finding itself on strange territory and deprived of its *manada*, the stallion would be more amenable to Colin's society.

"I'll go back on the rim, *amigo*," the Kid said quietly, closing the gate behind Colin and Mogollon. "You need help, I'll get back *pronto*."

"Don't start shooting unless there's no other way," Colin requested.

Left to himself, Colin removed the reins from the hackamore. Mogollon stood quietly, displaying no fear. Whether the condition would continue when the brow-band was raised remained to be seen. Still talking in a soothing manner, Colin eased the band upward. Then he turned and walked warily to the fence. On the rim, the kid held his rifle ready for use. The precaution proved to be unnecessary. Snorting softly, the stallion swung and hobbled across to the stream. By the time Colin had joined the Kid, Mogollon had quenched his thirst and stood peacefully grazing. The two men exchanged glances of relief. So far Mogollon showed no sign of distress or fretting over its lost freedom.

"I think I'll make a start at blanket-training him this evening," Colin said.

"May as well," agreed the Kid. "He looks to be settling down all right."

"If the Apache trained him with a blanket, it should make my work easier."

"Or harder. Depends on how the buck treated him."

After setting up their camp, Colin took a blanket and returned to the corral. Rifle in hand, the Kid flattened himself down on the rim. All too well the dark youngster knew the danger Colin faced. Maybe Mogollon had once been broken and trained, but several years of wild living might have destroyed its respect for human beings. Even with its fore legs hobbled, the *manadero* would be a formidable beast should it decide to attack the Scot.

Mogollon faced Colin, snorting and wary, but making no move to flee or charge. Back in the days when it had been owned by the Apache, it had learned not to fight against a rope or hobbles. Being choked down by the two Texans had revived memories of those days. There had been other treatment, equally painful, inflicted on it until it had learned to respond to its master's wishes.

Slowly Colin advanced, moving the blanket leisurely, but erratically in front of him. He had seen the Kid and the *mesteneros* use similar tactics on mustangs and had tried them himself with satisfactory results.

"Hoh! Shuh! Hoh! Shuh!" Colin grunted the traditional "horse talk" from deep in his chest. "Hoh! Hoh! Shuh! Shuh!"

All the time, Colin drew closer to Mogollon. The Kid's right eye squinted along the Winchester's twenty-six inch octagonal barrel, as he aligned its sights on the white star in the center of the horse's forehead.

Usually there would have been four men holding the horse while a "ghost cord" served as a further inducement to good behavior. By tying a thin rawhide cord about the horse's tongue and gums, the man doing the breaking could inflict pain as a punishment for disobedience. When the horse failed to respond, a tug on the cord stabbed agony through it. The method brought results, but often turned the suffering animal into a savage fighter. So Colin refused to use a ghost cord. He hoped to dominate Mogollon with firm, understanding kindness. Using "blanket" training offered him his best chance of doing it.

Continuing the monotonous "horse talk" and passes with the blanket, Colin held Mogollon's attention. Without hurry or fuss, he came close enough to place the blanket against the stallion's nostrils. Being one taken from Colin's bed, the blanket was impregnated with his scent. After allowing the horse to sniff at the material, he edged himself around to the side of its head. Mogollon snorted and stamped its hind feet, but neither backed away nor tried to attack Scot.

Still talking, Colin gripped the blanket between his knees and began to massage the stallion's body with his hands. When he saw that Mogollon allowed him to do so, he retrieved the blanket and started to waft it repeatedly on to the horse's back. When he laid the blanket on to Mogollon's back, the stallion grunted indignantly and tried to buck it off. The hobbles caused it to stumble. Instantly Colin whipped away the blanket, steadying and soothing the horse. Another session of massage and gentle swishing with the blanket restored Mogollon's confidence. When the Scot placed the blanket on the stallion's back for the second time, it stood quietly and made no attempt to throw off the light burden. With that much achieved, Colin retreated from the corral.

"He's taking it well so far," the Scot remarked as he returned to the Kid.

"Why sure," the youngster replied. "Looks like he remembers how he was trained. Was I you, though, I'd sleep outside the corral tonight."

"It might be as well," Colin admitted, for he would make his bed close to the stallion during the period of winning its confidence.

Arriving with food for the two men, Jeanie listened to Colin's glowing account of how the "blanket" training had progressed. With his meal eaten and Jeanie seen on her way, Colin took his bed roll to the corral. Although Mogollon stayed on the far side of the enclosure at first, it moved in Colin's direction after the Scot had settled down in his blankets. Lying without a movement, he saw the bulk of the stallion loom through the darkness. Mogollon advanced cautiously, ears pricked and nostrils testing the air. Colin made no attempt to rise nor speak, but remained perfectly still. Lowering its head, Mogollon sniffed through the rails of the corral at the motionless figure.

A feeling of contentment filled Colin, brought about

by the knowledge that Mogollon was his. In the morning he would continue with the "blanket" training, going through the various stages until he achieved his desires. Once Mogollon allowed the blanket to remain on its back, he would rest his elbows upon it, raise his feet and let the horse grow gradually accustomed to accepting his weight. When the time came for the first try at riding astride the stallion, he would lead it belly-deep into a pool along the stream. There Mogollon's ability to pitch and buck would be restricted and any throw Colin took would result in a ducking rather than a serious injury.

According to the Kid, if all went well the "blanket" training system accustomed the horse to a rider's weight and reduced bucking to a minimum. With Mogollon broken to the saddle, Colin could call himself a mustanger. He would also be able to use the stallion as a stud when he and Jeanie settled down on their ranch.

Still making plans for the future, with Mogollon standing close by on the other side of the fence, Colin drifted off to sleep.

CHAPTER NINE

The rumbling of many hooves mingled with the occasional crack of a shot, caused Colin Farquharson to bring Mogollon to a halt. Reaching forward and down, he slid his Henry rifle from its saddleboot. After throwing the lever through its loading cycle, he started the horse moving. Coming to the top of the slope up which he had been riding, he peered cautiously over. What he saw brought a grunt of annoyance and he returned the rifle to the boot.

Ten days had gone by since Mogollon's capture. Solitude and finding itself in a strange locale had rapidly won over the stallion. The "blanket" training had produced results which Colin had found most satisfying and all had gone as he had hoped it would. The fact that Mogollon had once been broken for riding had done much to reduce the task. Firmness and kindness had done the rest. By the fourth day, he had the horse accustomed to blanket and saddle. Two days later he had ridden Mogollon on dry land for the first time. After that, there had been a growing confidence between the Scot and the *manadero*.

So far Colin had not started to train Mogollon for any specialized type of work. Instead he intended to use it when scouting for other mustangs. That required no particular skills on the stallion's part, but permitted a greater understanding to develop between it and the Scot. After discussion with Jeanie, Colin had decided to wait until they had filled the orders for the OD Connected and the Army before commencing Mogollon's higher education.

What Colin saw as he topped the rim told him that the chances of locating *manadas* in its vicinity were being ruined. While he had never seen the type of activity being carried out before him, he had heard his companions talk of it. Now he could understand why the *mesteneros* had cursed its consequences with regard to their work.

Flanked by four fast-moving riders, a small herd of buffalo was racing along the level ground at the foot of the gentle slope beyond the rim. Growling his indignation, Colin studied them. Going by appearances, they "ran" the buffalo for sport rather than to collect meat or hides. That fact increased his antipathy toward them.

At the rear on the side closest to Colin rode a young U.S. Cavalry lieutenant holding a Henry rifle. On the opposite side of the herd, the second man's buckskin clothing and gunbelt with an open-topped holster hinted that he might be an Indian-scout or professional hunter. Up front, ahead of the hunter, a slender man dressed in Eastern riding fashion aimed a Spencer carbine from close range at a buffalo. Also dressed stylishly and Eastern, the fourth member of the party was a beautiful, black-haired woman. She too held a Spencer carbine. Raking her spurs along her horse's ribs, she goaded it to greater efforts in her attempt to catch up with the leaders of the herd.

Colin was less interested in the composition of the party than with how their "running" the buffalo herd—seeing how many they could shoot on the move—would affect the mustanging prospects. Another good *corrida* would see the OD Connected's requirements satisfied and the Army's contract well on the way to completion. That would not be possible in the surrounding country for some time to come. Even if the wild horses were not driven out of the vicinity, they would be extra wary and alert after such a scare.

Just before coming level with Colin's position, the male Easterner's carbine cracked. Caught from a range hardly exceeding two feet, the buffalo in front of the muzzle swerved violently. Its legs buckled and it went down. In falling, its actions startled the animal at which the woman was lining her weapon.

Even as Béatrice, Vicomtesse de Brioude, squeezed her borrowed carbine's trigger, she saw the buffalo at which she was aiming suddenly alter direction. Flame licked from the Spencer's barrel. Instead of driving into the animal's ribcage, the bullet tore a furrow across its hump. Cutting loose with a shrill, enraged hiss that sounded like steam being released under high pressure from an engine, the wounded beast turned and lunged toward its assailant.

Being trained for buffalo running, Béatrice's horse knew the danger. Instead of allowing it to avoid the charge, she tried to guide it in what would have been the wrong direction. With a squeal, the bay gelding took the bit between its teeth and hurtled forward. Left to its own devices, it would have carried them both to safety. Béatrice's intervention delayed it for long enough to put them in a dangerous situation.

Finding that its victim was spurting clear, the buffalo essayed a quick hook which spiked the tip of its horn into the bay's rump. Again the horse squealed. More pained than hurt, it flung itself onward at an even greater speed. Being completely surprised by the sudden increase in motion, Béatrice almost went flying from the saddle. Thrown forward, she dropped the Spencer. Up flew her hands, letting the reins fall, and her feet flapped to the rear. The screech she let out did nothing to lessen the bay's pace. With the bit gripped firmly in its teeth, it raced away from the herd. Instead of retrieving the reins from the horse's neck and using them to control it, she clung to the saddlehorn with both hands. Finding itself free from restraint, the bay followed its natural inclination to put as much distance as possible between itself and the buffalo.

Seeing Béatrice's horse bolting, Lieutenant Lebel swerved away from the rear of the herd and gave chase. Abe Peet, the hunter, took one glance in her direction and swung his mount behind the last of the buffalo. Not a bad-looking man, Peet had received sufficient encourage-

ment from the Vicomtesse to figure rescuing her would
bring a satisfactory reward. He did not want the
bow-necked officer to be the one who received it.

Watching the men, Colin realized that neither of them
sat a horse capable of overtaking the bay quickly. Maybe
they could not even catch the frightened animal. If so, the
woman might be carried for miles. Even worse, in her
panic she might fall off. At the speed her mount was
running, that would be very dangerous.

Nudging Mogollon's ribs gently with his heels, Colin
set the stallion into motion. From the four-beat gait of a
collected walk, his further heel and rein signals induced
Mogollon to open out into a gallop. He felt the mighty
body between his legs change its easy movements to a
powerful, pulsating thrust as it increased its speed.
Settling into the heels-down, toes-in, leg position, Colin
thrust his shoulders forward and chest out. Unlike
Béatrice, he retained his hold on the reins and so could
keep the stallion under control. Beneath them, the ground
was ideally suited for galloping; firm but not so hard that
it threw undue pressure on the frogs of the hooves. Nor
did the gentle slope pose any serious threat, for Mogollon
had the agility of a cat over that kind of surface. So the
stallion sped on a converging course with Béatrice's bay.
It moved with the flashing speed that had so often carried
it to safety when chased by human pursuers.

Becoming aware of his wife's predicament, the
Vicomte de Brioude reined in his horse. While waiting for
the buffalo herd to stream by him, his attention
transformed from Béatrice to Colin. Stiffening in his
saddle and restraining his mount, de Brioude stared in
awe at the manner in which the great chestnut stallion was
racing in the Vicomtesse's direction.

Fright had added speed to the bay gelding's flight and
Béatrice's behavior did not improve matters. Clinging
desperately to the saddlehorn, swaying from side to side,
she repeatedly screamed in a manner calculated to keep
the horse running. All the wild exhilaration of the chase
had left her and she felt only raw fear.

Fast though the bay moved, it could not match the controlled speed of the chestnut stallion. With each sequence of the galloping gait's hoof-beats, Mogollon lessened the distance between them. Seeing the gap closing brought up a problem for Colin. How could he save the woman once he reached her?

Trying to rope the gelding offered no solution, Mogollon lacked the training necessary for such work. Nor did Colin think much of his chances if he tried to come alongside the woman's horse, lean over and grab at the reins or headstall. While his riding skill would be equal to the task, any slight mistake on his part or panic by the woman could throw the bay off balance with fatal consequences for her. As far as Colin could see, there was only one way that he might effect the rescue. It would be as risky as hell, but better than any of the other means which had occurred to him.

Drawing level with the woman, Colin began to edge Mogollon closer to the bay. He saw a beautiful face, distorted by fear, turn toward him.

"Help me!" Béatrice screeched, speaking French in her fright.

There was no time for Colin to say anything comforting, nor to discuss his plan for her salvation. Already the gelding showed signs of moving away from what might be a source of further pain and danger. Mogollon still remained under Colin's control, striding out fast and ignoring the other horse. Gripping the reins in his left hand, Colin steered his mount until his right leg almost brushed against the hem of Béatrice's divided skirt.

"Get your feet out of the stirrups!" Colin snapped, hoping that she retained sufficient sense to obey.

Making sure of his balance on the saddle, he leaned over and hooked his right arm about Béatrice's waist. Immediately he sensed rather than saw the bay veering away and felt its rider being drawn from its back. Moaning in terror, Béatrice locked her arms around his neck in a vice-like grip. Colin felt a momentary surge of concern. Unless she had heard and obeyed him, they would be in deadly peril. He doubted if she would release her hold no matter what the consequences.

The gelding continued to move away. Still supported by his arm and clinging to Colin's neck, the woman parted company with it. Whether she had heard his instructions, or had already lost her stirrup irons, Colin could not guess. Whichever reason, she had left the bay and not become entangled with the stirrups. With her body dangling from him, Colin devoted his whole attention to bringing Mogollon to a halt. He was not helped any by her wildly kicking legs, or arms clinging to his neck and half strangling him.

"You can let go now, ma'am," Colin gritted as he finally stopped the stallion. "It's all right. You're safe enough now."

With that, he bent over and lowered her feet to the ground. For a moment she retained her hold, then opened her arms and stepped away. Colin had thought her to be beautiful during his earlier, brief glimpses. Taking his first uninterrupted look at her, he decided that he had never seen a more seductively attractive woman. That feeling increased when, after a few seconds, the fear left her features. Staring up, her eyes roved over him.

"You saved my life!" Béatrice purred, studying her rescuer with an expression that went beyond the bonds of gratitude.

Brought about by the Vicomtesse's predatory scrutiny, an uneasy sensation bit into Colin. However, before any more could be said, the young officer arrived and brought his horse to a rump-sliding halt. An instant later, while Lebel was still throwing himself from his saddle, Peet thundered up. The newcomers' eyes swung from Béatrice to Colin. Conscious of their cold scowls, the Scot figured that his intervention had not been welcomed by either man and could guess why. Béatrice was dressed as she had been on her first meeting with Mark. Although her glove hid the wedding ring, Colin felt sure that she would never allow a minor detail like having a husband interfere with her dealings with other men.

"Are you all right, Béatrice?" Lebel gasped, concern showing on his face. Since leaving Fort Sawyer, his scruples about love-making with a married woman had been reduced and he was completely infatuated by the Vicomtesse.

"You're safe, thank God!" Peet barked, leaping from his mount and letting it stand with trailing reins.

"Thanks to this gentleman I am!" Béatrice replied coldly. "Perhaps one of you can manage to catch my horse."

"Go and get it, Peet!" Lebel ordered.

"Go fetch it yourself, blue-belly!" the hunter spat back. "I ain't in the blasted Army so I—"

"Don't start bickering!" Béatrice commanded, the thought of the narrowly averted danger putting a sharp edge in her voice. "I want my horse collected. Right now!"

"I'll go for it," Peet offered. "The luff'll[1] likely get his-self all lost if he went off without somebody to hold his hand."

"That damned, no-account—!" the officer began, glaring at Peet's departing back then becoming aware that Béatrice was paying no attention to his words.

"Sacred mother!" the Vicomtesse ejaculated in French, staring at Mogollon. "Never have I seen such a magnificent horse."

At that moment, her husband arrived. Looking at the slender, dandified figure, Colin formed the impression that he was displaying more interest in Mogollon than toward the woman. With an effort, de Brioude diverted his gaze from the stallion to Béatrice.

"You are all right, *cherie*?" the Vicomte asked.

"Shaken up a little," Béatrice replied, "but nothing worse."

"You saved my wife's life, *m'sieur*," de Brioude went on, turning to Colin. "None of us has a mount that could have caught her horse so quickly."

"This horse of mine's not slow," Colin conceded.

"Not slow?" repeated Béatrice, walking forward and

---

[1]Luff: a derogatory name for a 1st lieutenant.

extending her right hand. "Why he must run like the—"

"Don't touch him, ma'am!" Colin warned as Mogollon snorted and swung his head toward the woman in a threatening manner the Scot had come to recognize. "He doesn't take kindly to strangers handling him."

"May I ask my rescuer's name?" Béatrice inquired, lowering her hand.

"Yes, *m'sieur*," de Brioude went on. "A rescuer arriving at such an opportune moment is surprising enough. But a Scot wearing a kilt—"

"My name's Colin Farquharson—"

"Aren't you the feller who's working for Libby Schell?" Lebel interrupted, deciding that an answer in the affirmative would change Béatrice's feelings toward her rescuer.

"Aye, that I am," Colin confirmed.

Instantly he could sense the chill which came into Béatrice's manner. Then things began to slip into focus for him. On the night of their return from Fort Sawyer, Libby and Mark had told of the incidents at the hotel and store. The woman Colin had rescued must be the same who had caused Mark so much trouble. Clearly her feelings about Libby matched the blonde's antipathy toward her.

"Then you are a—how do you say it—mustanger, *m'sieur*?" de Brioude asked eagerly, ignoring his wife's change of attitude. "You catch, break and sell wild horses?"

"I help do it," Colin agreed.

"Will you sell the one you are riding to me?" de Brioude wanted to know.

"Yes, *m'sieur*," Béatrice put in. "Will you? I do so want it."

"I'm sorry, ma'am," Colin replied, noticing that a forced smile had come to Béatrice's lips. "Mogollon's not for sale."

"But, *m'sieur*," Béatrice purred seductively, "I do *so* want it. Surely *you* won't disappoint *me*?"

Behind the words lay an implied promise of benefits far greater than mere money. They hinted that Béatrice's gratitude would be well worth receiving. More than one man, faced with the full force of her voluptuous charm had yielded to her wishes or complied with her desires.

"It grieves me, ma'am, but I'll have to," Colin answered.

"But surely you can sell us the horse," Béatrice insisted in her most winning manner. "As a favor to *me*. My husband will let you name your own price."

"Money doesn't come into it, ma'am," Colin explained. "I caught Mogollon as a wedding gift for my fiancée. So, you see, I couldn't sell him."

"But surely you have other horses," the Vicomtesse pouted, trying to hide her true feelings.

"There's only one Mogollon, ma'am," Colin declared. "I'm sorry, but I can't sell him. Well, seeing that you're safe, I'd best be on my way."

Anybody who knew Béatrice would have read a warning from the way her eyes narrowed and the pout disappeared to turn her full lips into a tight line. Those were signs that her temper approached its boiling point. In addition to anger at having her desires disregarded, she had another reason for wanting the horse.

Already impressed by Mogollon's size, beauty and presence, learning why Colin would not sell had increased Béatrice's determination to obtain the horse. The Vicomtesse could not forget how Libby Schell had thwarted her plans regarding Mark Counter. Brooding on the result of the affair, Béatrice had turned much of her hate from the blond giant to Libby. If the fat old bitch had not been with him, Béatrice felt certain that *le beau* Counter would have rushed willingly into her arms. Discovering that Libby had been in Mark's bed had increased the Vicomtesse's hatred. Now she could see a way of avenging herself. Maybe the old woman was the fiancée for whom the stallion was intended. If so, forcing the Scot to sell it would be the more satisfactory.

"Wait, *M'sieur* Farquharson!" de Brioude said, cutting through his wife's thought train as the Scot started to turn away. "I beg you to reconsider—"

"There's nothing to reconsider," Colin cut in coldly,

then relented a little. "If you come to our camp on Wolf Creek, we can offer you a couple of young stallions sired by him."

"I want that horse!" Béatrice spat out. "No other will do."

"Like I said, ma'am," Colin answered. "He's not for sale. *Adios*."

"Can't you make him sell it to me, Charles?" Béatrice demanded, swinging to face the officer as Colin rode away.

"I've no authority to make him sell," Lebel replied, looking uncomfortable.

Since leaving Fort Sawyer, the lieutenant had learned that Béatrice hated to be refused anything. Giving Lebel a glare that carried a knife-like cutting edge, she spun toward her husband.

"I want that horse, Arnaud!"

"Of course you do, *cherie*," de Brioude said soothingly, flickering a glance at Lebel and making a small signaling motion with his head.

"Charles," Béatrice purred, knowing what her husband meant. "I dropped my carbine when the horse bolted. Be a darling and fetch it for me."

"Sure, Béatrice," Lebel agreed, only too pleased to get away.

"I'm determined to have that horse," Béatrice stated, after the officer had ridden out of hearing. "I don't care how you do it, Arnaud, but I *will* have it."

"And I intend to see that you get it, *cherie*," de Brioude promised.

"Is this eagerness just to please me?" Béatrice asked suspiciously.

"I *always* try to please you."

"Especially when there's something in it for you. What is it this time?"

"I saw how fast that horse can run. It caught up to your bay as if you'd been standing still. There's much money to be made, racing and betting on such a horse, *cherie*."

"You'll have to get it first," Béatrice warned.

"I intend to do that," de Brioude assured her and

looked at Peet as he returned leading the bay. "Do you know that mustanger, Abe?"

"I've heard tell of him," the hunter replied. "Way he's dressed, I'd say he's the one who works for Libby Schell 'n' took out the Flores boys—"

"I want that horse he is riding, Abe," Béatrice interrupted in her most winning manner. "Arnaud tried to buy it, but he wouldn't sell."

"Maybe you didn't offer him enough money, Arnaud," Peet suggested.

"Béatrice told him he could name his own price," de Brioude stated. "He still refused to sell."

"Did, huh?" grunted the hunter, guessing at the way the conversation headed. "That looks like the end of it then."

"People sometimes change their minds," de Brioude pointed out. "Especially if they—shall we say—have help to make them change."

"Happen you're figuring on doing the making, the blue-belly there won't stand for it," warned Peet, nodding in Lebel's direction.

"He doesn't have to know," Béatrice pointed out, laying a hand on Peet's thigh. "Abe, I'll be *so* grateful to the man who gets me that horse."

"You minding how it's got?" the hunter inquired, leaning forward to tap the butt of his long-barreled Sharps rifle.

"We don't care," Béatrice declared.

"Just make sure that you don't bring the police around us," de Brioude went on. "Can you do it?"

"Easy," Peet grinned. "I'll cover my tracks so nobody can follow 'em and hide the hoss someplace until it's safe to bring him to you."

"Can we do anything to help?" asked de Brioude.

"Call off the hunting for today 'n' take Lebel back to camp with you," Peet advised. "I'll make out I'm going to scout for another buffler herd so's I don't need to come along."

Although the de Brioudes did as their hunter requested, Peet failed to achieve anything. By the time he had come into rifle range of Colin, two *mesteneros* had joined the Scot. So Peet called off his attempt to obtain the stallion by the simple means of shooting its rider. Having come to know his employers pretty well, he doubted if they would be content to let the matter rest there.

CHAPTER TEN

Holding their mounts to a leisurely walk, Dusty Fog and Colin Farquharson passed through an area of woodland and came into sight of Kerrville about a mile to the south.

"Not a mustang, much less a *manada* or *mestena* down this way," Colin remarked, stroking Mogollon's neck. "Libby won't be pleased when she hears about it."

"Likely," Dusty admitted. "Only we don't know that it's those French folk's hunting that's scared them away. This section's a mite too close to the town for mustangs to use it."

A point with which Colin agreed. He hoped that Libby would be of the same opinion. There had been an explosive scene at their camp when Libby Schell had heard about Colin's meeting with the Vicomtesse de Brioude. Learning that Béatrice was a member of the hunting party, Libby had blamed it for the shortage of *manadas* on that section of the range. Only by exercising considerable tact had Dusty and Colin dissuaded the blonde from gathering her *mesteneros* and attempting to carry out her threat of chasing the French couple into the sea at Brownsville.

That had been three days ago. Despite knowing that the area down toward Kerrville rarely held mustangs, Libby had insisted that it be thoroughly scouted for them. After helping with the gelding of the captured stock and other work, the two young men had agreed to make a final check of the area. By that time Libby's temper had cooled down somewhat and the situation at the camp was returning to normal. Colin hoped that nothing would happen to change the cooling-down process.

"Why don't we ride in and see Cousin Tam?" the Scot suggested.

"We might as well," Dusty agreed, guiding his *bayo-cebrunos* gelding in the required direction. "Happen he'll ride out to supper with us, Libby might forget the de Brioudes."

By the time they had covered half of the distance to the town, Dusty and Colin had become aware of its deserted appearance. Three men crossed the main street and entered one of its largest buildings, but apart from them there was little or no sign of human life. Going closer, the two riders noticed some activity around the combined church and meeting house on the far side of town.

"Could be trouble," Dusty said when Colin commented on the town's deserted aspect. "Everything looks to be closed up for the day."

"If it is trouble, Cousin Tam might need help," the Scot answered. "I wonder where we'll find him?"

"At the jailhouse, likely," Dusty guessed. "If he's not, the owner of the livery barn might know where he's at."

Entering town, they found the jailhouse devoid of life. So they made their way toward the open main doors of the livery barn. Approaching the building into which the three men had disappeared, Dusty noticed that it was the Logan Hotel.

"We could go in and ask about Tam," the small Texan said.

"I'd rather leave Mogollon in a stall than on a hitching rail," Colin replied. "He's not used to being in a town."

On reaching the livery barn, they dismounted and led the horses inside. All but two of the stalls had occupants, but the owner and his assistants were conspicuous by their absence.

"What do we do now?" Colin asked.

"Put up the horses," Dusty answered. "Then we'll go find out what's happening around here."

Taking their mounts into the empty stalls, Dusty and Colin prepared to settle them in. Footsteps drew their attention to the rear entrance. A tall, heavily built, genial-featured man came in. Bare-footed, he wore jeans and an undershirt. Although Colin had not previously visited the town, the man showed only momentary surprise at being confronted by a kilted Scot.

"Howdy, gents," the newcomer greeted. "You'll be Tam Breda's kinsman, I reckon. I've heard tell about them fancy duds you wear. Say, if you're looking for Tam, he's took a posse down south after a bunch of *bandidos*."

"So that's where all the men-folk've gone," Dusty put in.

"Some of 'em're with Tam," admitted the owner. "I reckon the rest're like me."

"How'd that be?" Dusty inquired.

"Getting ready for this here fancy ree-ception the mayor 'n' city fathers're throwing for the French count and countess who've bought the old Renfrew place to start up ranching."

Colin threw a startled glance Dusty's way. It seemed that the de Brioudes were going out of their way to antagonize Libby Schell. Agreeing with Colin's views on the decrease of mustanging prospects in the future, Libby had suggested that, on the completion of the Army remount contract, they should purchase the Renfrew property as their horse ranch. Deserted during the War by its owners, it would have been well suited to the Schell family's needs.

"Damned if the women-folk ain't buzzing around like a humming-bird with six tails," the owner continued. "They're all a-hunting up fancy dresses and running us husbands ragged duding up for it. Which's why I wasn't here where I should be. The missus's had me a-shining boots and's making me take an all-over bath. Not's I mind. The Count's a real swell gent, and they do say his wife's a real looker. Tam Breda's grateful to the Count, I'll bet."

"How come?" Dusty asked.

"Like I said, word come in about this here *bandido* gang rampaging down south. Tam's not got his-self settled in and hired enough men to handle it. Anyways, him, the marshal 'n' some of us was fixing to ride when damned if the count don't come in and offer to lend Tam his whole Army escort."

"That was good of him," Colin said sincerely.

"We thought so," the owner replied. "Anyways, the mayor 'n' city fathers figured we should make him and his missus welcome. So we asked 'em to come in today for what Annie Logan calls a ree-ception." A faint grin creased his face and he went on, "Looks like Annie don't write French's good's she allows. The count and his missus've come in early. That sort of put the committee fixing the shin-dig in a mite of a fix."

"Henry!" screeched an irate female voice from somewhere behind the barn. "You get back here!"

"Look, gents," the owner said apologetically. "Everything you need's on hand. If you'll tend to things yourself, I'll be right obliged. Was you married, you'd—"

"Henry!" yelled the voice.

"We'll make out," Dusty assured the man.

"Thanks, fellers," Henry said and departed the way from which he had come.

"Now that's what you're letting yourself in for when you marry Jeanie," Dusty warned the Scot.

"I'll change i—" Colin began.

The arrival of a man through the front doors brought Colin's words to a halt. Turning his head, the Scot recognized the hunter who had been with the de Brioudes. Throwing a look at Dusty and clearly dismissing him as of no importance, Peet slouched across to the gate of Mogollon's stall.

"Howdy, friend," greeted the hunter. "Don't know if you 'member me or not. I was with that French countess you saved when her hoss bolted."

"I remember," Colin admitted.

"She's up to the hotel with her husband," Peet continued. "They done sent me to ask you to come and see 'em."

"Why?"

"They've been thinking, 'n' allow, seeing's you don't

aim to sell Mogollon there, they might's well buy some of his young 'n's."

For a moment Colin did not reply. Taking everything into consideration, he wondered if Libby would agree to selling horses to the de Brioudes. A glance showed the Scot that Dusty was going on tending to the *bayo-cebruno's* needs. Not that Colin intended to ask for help with his decision. To do so would lessen his standing in the *big*, efficient, self-reliant Texan's eyes.

"I'll be along as soon as I've seen to my horse," Colin promised, deciding that he would lose nothing by hearing what the Vicomte had to say.

"The count's got him a meeting with the local folks in half an hour or so," Peet remarked. "Until then he's down to the hotel. Folks're all staying clear, so you can talk private-like."

"Tell him I'll come as soon as I can," Colin suggested.

"I'll do that," Peet grunted and walked from the building.

Watching the hunter go, Dusty decided that he had been one of the three who had entered the hotel. That figured, seeing how he worked for the de Brioudes. Going by their dress, the other two had been cowhands. Either they were hired by the Vicomte, or soliciting employment. Before Dusty could comment on the matter, Colin swung in his direction.

"Did I do the right thing, Dusty?"

"How'd you mean?"

"By agreeing to go and see de Brioude. Libby might not want to do business with him."

"If he wants the horses, he'll likely be willing to pay higher than us or the Army for them," Dusty stated. "From what Mark said, he's rich and you'll get cash-money for them. And I'd bet Libby's too good a businesswoman to turn down a fair offer because she doesn't like the wife of the feller making it."

"I think you're right," Colin admitted and changed the subject. "Why do you think the local people are staying away from the de Brioudes? I'd have expected them to be gathering around."

"It figures in a way," Dusty replied. "The de Brioudes settling close by'll be a big help to Kerr County. They'll be needing supplies, fittings for the house, plenty of things and Kerrville's the closest place to get them."

"So I'd expect the local businessmen to be swarming around—"

"Likely the folks fixing up this reception figured the same way. But when the de Brioudes arrived early, they aimed to make sure that nobody gets a head start on the others with them. So they asked them to wait down to the hotel and all agreed to leave meeting 'em until the reception."

"You could be right," Colin grinned.

Suffering from the depression brought about by the War, the citizens of Kerrville would see the arrival of the de Brioudes as a blessing. So the leading members of the community had recognized the advisability of preventing a premature scramble to make their acquaintance. The danger of friction and unpleasantness had been removed by the practical means of everybody keeping away from the guests-of-honor until the actual ceremony commenced.

After completing the watering and feeding of their mounts, Dusty and Colin left the stalls. Fastening the gates, they took and hung their saddles on the inverted-V shaped wooden burro erected along one wall for that purpose.

"It was real good of de Brioude to loan his escort to Tam," Colin commented as he and Dusty left the barn.

"Or a right smart move," the small Texan replied. "Doing it set him up real good with the folks in town. Taken with the money he's likely to bring into Kerr County, it'll put them on his side happen anybody tries to make fuss for him."

"You mean they'd not take kindly to Libby doing anything that might chase the de Brioudes away?" Colin guessed.

"That's just what I mean," Dusty confirmed. "I know you were hoping to get that Renfrew place, but you'd best forget it if de Brioude's moved in."

"Libby won't like it," Colin said. "But she's too smart to do anything rash or foolish."

"I reckon she is," Dusty drawled.

On their arrival at the hotel, Dusty and Colin found Peet waiting in the hall with the de Brioudes. Smiling a welcome, the Vicomte advanced with his right hand held out toward the Scot. Dusty thought that the smile looked a little forced, then became aware of a change come over the Frenchman's face. What started out as a flickered look his way turned into a longer, closer scrutiny. It almost seemed that de Brioude saw beyond Dusty's small, insignificant outer shell and suspected something of the real man underneath.

"Ha! *M'sieur* Farquharson," the Vicomte said, jerking his eyes from Dusty and shaking hands with Colin. "I am so pleased that you could come to see me. If your friend doesn't mind, we'll go into the dining room and talk."

"I'm at your service, sir," Colin answered. "May I present Ca—"

"Good afternoon, young man," Béatrice put in, advancing with her most sensual glide and addressing Dusty. "My husband and I wish to speak privately with *M'sieur* Farquharson. I am sure you won't mind waiting in the barroom?"

Studying the Vicomtesse, Dusty decided that Mark had not exaggerated when describing her physical attractions. Nor, in Dusty's opinion, did Libby go far out in her uncomplimentary assessment of Béatrice's character. There was an underlying hardness about the woman which hinted at a harsh, intolerant disregard for others, determination to have all things her own way and latent snobbery. No matter how her husband felt about the small Texan, she clearly dismissed him as an unimportant, inconsiderable nobody unfit to be in her company.

"But this—!" Colin spluttered, annoyed by the Vicomtesse's treatment of a friend.

"It's all right, Colin," Dusty interrupted cheerfully. "I know how it is. You go talk your business. I'll have a beer while I'm waiting."

"You may tell the—how do you say—bartender to charge your drinks to my husband," Béatrice purred, in a way calculated to charm a naïve country boy and make him subservient to her will.

"Of course you may," de Brioude confirmed, still darting puzzled and worried looks from Colin to Dusty.

"Come, *m'sieur*," Béatrice said, laying a hand on Colin's sleeve. "Let us see what kind of a horse-trade—don't you call it?—we can make."

Gripping Colin's arm, and giving him no opportunity to complete his introduction of Dusty, the Vicomtesse led him into the small dining room at the left of the hall. For a moment de Brioude seemed to be on the verge of speaking to Dusty. Deciding against it, the Vicomte went after Colin and his wife. Eyeing Dusty's gunbelt with the kind of mocking amusement that the small Texan had seen on other faces, until he had been given cause to draw the Colts, Peet followed the others.

Watching them go, Dusty smiled sardonically. During the War, he had met several members of the European aristocracy, either as combatants or military observers. Accustomed to the near-feudal class distinctions of their society—as strong in the French Republic as elsewhere in the Old World—they had often failed to appreciate that more free-and-easy conditions prevailed upon the United States' Western frontiers. So he felt neither surprised nor annoyed at the de Brioudes' behavior toward him.

Regarding Dusty as a mere employee—and probably not an important one at that—the de Brioudes did not want him around while they talked business with Colin. Although the Vicomte had hidden his feelings, his wife made no attempt to do so. Dusty felt relieved that he had not been introduced. If Colin had done so, it might have been an embarrassment for all concerned. Learning Dusty's identity would have most likely changed the de Brioudes' feelings and caused them to invite him to join them. After which, if either of them had asked Dusty's advice, his answer might be detrimental to Colin's trading.

All in all, Dusty decided that he was better off unrecognized and waiting in the barroom until a deal had been concluded. Then, if Colin felt so inclined, he could perform the introduction and most likely hand the de Brioude family something of a surprise.

On entering the dining room, Béatrice directed Colin to a table covered with a white lace cloth probably brought out by the owner in honor of her visit. Crossing to the window, Peet leaned his shoulder on the wall and looked out. The hunter's presence did little to relieve Colin's annoyance at how the de Brioudes had treated Dusty. Obviously they regarded Peet as suitable to listen to their business. Possibly they felt that they might need the hunter's specialized knowledge, which was understandable.

Turning his attention fully to the Vicomtesse as she asked if he would care for a drink or anything to eat, Colin decided that she had taken care with her appearance. Under the black top hat, with its silken retaining band extending to her waist, her hair looked perfectly groomed and face faultlessly if tactfully painted and powdered. Her snow white blouse and black riding habit exhibited her physical attractions without being blatant. Diamonds decorated her wrists and fingers.

After Colin had declined Béatrice's offer, de Brioude made no attempt to start discussing business. Instead he repeated his thanks for Colin saving his wife and commented on Mogollon's excellence. Colin sensed an air of tension shared by the other occupants of the room and wondered at its cause.

Could it be that de Brioude had got Colin alone to try to force him into selling Mogollon?

That seemed highly unlikely. Perhaps Peet did not know Dusty Fog, or recognize the small Texan's potential, but he would be unlikely to be party to such a scheme. Nor would de Brioude contemplate making the attempt, even with the favor of Kerrville's citizens swinging his way.

Yet there was something. Just what, Colin could not decide. As if becoming aware of the Scot's thoughts, Béatrice put on her most charming manner.

"And do you plan to make Texas your home, *m'sieur*?" she inquired.

"Aye, that I do, ma'am," Colin replied and turned to her husband. "I don't want to sound impertinent, sir, but you have this reception soon and Captain Fog's waiting in the bar for me."

"Cap'n Fog!" Peet yelped, thrusting himself away from the wall. "You mean that short—that—the feller who was with you's Dusty Fog?"

"He is," Colin agreed.

"Dusty Fog!" the Vicomte croaked, staring at the door.

"Mon Dieu!" Béatrice gasped, almost at the same moment.

Only by making an effort did Colin keep his face impassive and hide the amusement he felt at the surprise shown by the de Brioudes and Peet. Having seen several people's reactions at discovering that the short cowhand was the legendary Dusty Fog, he found nothing unusual in their startled exclamations.

"You ain't joshing us?" Peet demanded, crossing the room.

"If you think that," Colin replied calmly, "go over to the bar and ask him."

"Hell!" ejaculated the hunter, glaring as he meant to follow the Scot's suggestion. "Then—!"

"Arnaud!" Béatrice said loudly, chopping off the hunter's words. "What must Captain Fog think of us, acting as we did?"

"We must make amends!" de Brioude went on. "Abe, would you go and ask Captain Fog if he will join us?"

At that moment, the crackle of gunfire sounded from across the hall. The barroom lay in that direction, so Colin did not hesitate. Drawing his Dragoon, he sprang to and jerked open the door. Followed by Peet, the Scot darted across the hall.

CHAPTER ELEVEN

Entering the barroom of the Logan Hotel, Dusty found its only occupants to be a slim, cold-eyed gambler seated at a table on the side facing the door and a bulky, surly featured hard-case in cowhand clothing lounging at each end of the counter. They were the two men who had accompanied the hunter into the building. If he had recommended either man to the de Brioudes, the hunter possessed mighty poor judgment or some ulterior motive for doing it. No matter how they dressed, Dusty doubted if the pair had ever worked cattle on a ranch. However, it was none of Dusty's affair.

"Howdy," Dusty greeted, crossing to the center of the bar. "Isn't anybody serving, gents?"

"It sure as hell don't look that way," the man at the right side answered.

If Mark Counter or Tam Breda had been present, they would have identified all three men. While Dusty had heard Mark mention Stagge, Coxin and Royce, he failed to identify them from his *amigo's* brief, unflattering descriptions. The absence of Laura and the small man deprived Dusty of clues that might otherwise have helped him.

"You don't need no barkeep anyways," Coxin declared, from Dusty's left and eyed him with disdain. "They don't serve no hard liquor to frying-sized half-portions like you."

"Milk'd be more your needings, short stuff," Royce scoffed.

111

"They do say milk never hurt anybody, mister," Dusty remarked quietly.

"And what's that supposed to mean?" Royce demanded, advancing along the bar in a threatening manner.

Despite sensing the two hard-cases' hostility, Dusty made no attempt to leave the room. His every instinct told him that they were on the prod and determined to make trouble for somebody. Experience with their kind in the Army and since the end of the War had taught him that backing down would solve nothing. Revising his opinion, Dusty classified them as small-town loafers and bullies. Probably their arrival at the same time as the hunter had been no more than coincidence, for seeking regular employment rarely fitted into such men's ways.

Deprived of drinks by the bartender's absence, the pair most likely wanted somebody on whom they could work out their spite. Probably they had figured the gambling man to be too tough a proposition. It would be in keeping with their sort's habits to pick on a small, unoffending and apparently harmless young stranger. If that was the case, Dusty reckoned they had made a mighty poor choice by selecting him as their victim.

"I didn't come in here looking for fuss," Dusty warned gently, swinging so that he placed his back to the bar. "So let's forget the whole thing."

Dusty spoke in a tone of voice that the enlisted men of Company "C" and the OD Connected's cowhands had come to know and respect as a danger signal. When he used it, wise men hunted for the storm-shelters or made good and certain that they respected his wishes.

Failing to identify Dusty, so not knowing his ways, Coxin and Royce continued to move in his direction. While Royce held the small Texan's attention from the right, Coxin glided closer as silently as he could manage. Aware of his companion's ability in a roughhouse brawl, Royce was content to keep back and let Coxin make the opening attack.

Lulled into a sense of false security by Dusty's small size and general air of unpreparedness, Coxin took a step away from the bar and shot out his hands. He clamped a hold on the front of Dusty's shirt and left bicep, preparing to swing him bodily into the center of the room. To Coxin, there seemed no way in which his victim could avoid what he planned. Ignorance concerning the "victim," especially of one aspect, was about to cost the hard-case dearly.

Down in the Rio Hondo, a short Oriental man worked as Ole Devil Hardin's personal servant. Tommy Okasi claimed to be Nipponese and possessed devastatingly effective methods of bare-handed fighting. To Dusty, smallest male member of the Hardin, Fog and Blaze clan, the little servant had passed on a thorough working knowledge of *ju-jitsu* and *karate*. Those techniques, hardly known at that time outside the Japanese Empire, had helped Dusty to earn his reputation for defeating larger, heavier and stronger men.

Allowing Coxin to reach him "undetected" and take hold, Dusty based his line of action on what the other planned to do. Blending his movements with the hard-case's lifting pull, Dusty twisted his hips and torso to the left. At the same moment he swung his free hand up and around so that it passed above his assailant's arms. Extending his right arm, Dusty kept his hand open and fingers outstretched but together. The manner in which he struck at Coxin might have looked strange, awkward even, to Occidental eyes, but proved to be most effective. Dusty had learned from Tommy Okasi that the extended fingers, heel or edge of the hand could serve just as well as the knuckles when wielded correctly.

Although done with great accuracy, Dusty's attack was not preformed at anything like his best speed. He needed Coxin to realize at which point he was aiming his hand. Becoming aware of the target as Dusty's finger tips raked across his eyes, Coxin started to draw back his face. Pain and an instinctive desire to protect his sight caused the hard-case to tilt his torso and snap his head hurriedly to the rear.

Having brought about the required reaction, Dusty clenched his fist and bent his right arm. Again he did not use his knuckles. Instead, he hurled his arm so that the point of its elbow rammed with considerable force into Coxin's *solar plexus*. A startled, agonized croak burst from the hard-case as the blow landed and he opened his hands. As he struck, Dusty had already started to swing his left shoulder away and wrench his arm from Coxin's grasp. Liberated, he carried his left hand, folded into a fist, until it rested against his near hip.

Dusty's response and its result had come almost as much of a surprise to Royce as it had to its recipient. Clenching his hard fists, Royce advanced at a better pace in the hope of taking Dusty while the small Texan was still occupied by Coxin. Royce's hope met with disillusionment.

Alert for danger from the second man, Dusty threw a quick glance across his left shoulder. Quick, maybe, but telling him all he needed to know. Grasping and clutching at his body where the elbow had impacted, Coxin staggered backwards sufficiently for Dusty to have room to maneuver. Figuring to take advantage of his extra reach, Royce hurled a punch while still at arm's length from the small Texan. Dusty bent his right knee slightly and took his full weight on that foot. Drawing his other leg up, he inclined his body away from Royce and hurled his left foot to the rear. Carried on by the impetus of his blow, Royce took the high heel of Dusty's boot full in the pit of the stomach.

From delivering the snap kick, which halted Royce in his tracks, Dusty dropped his left foot to the floor and used it as a pivot to run on his second attacker. Royce had not even had time to lower his right arm from its abortive punch. Stabbing out his left hand, Dusty shoved Royce's fist aside. Using his pivot to add force to it, Dusty whipped his right arm around and delivered an open-palm slap to the side of Royce's head. The power behind the blow spun the burly hard-case toward the center of the room.

Thrusting himself away from the confines of the bar, Dusty moved toward the door and halted facing the hard-cases. He threw a look at the gambler, finding the other sat staring as if unwilling to believe the evidence of his eyes. Then Dusty gave his attention to Coxin and Royce.

"All right," the small Texan growled. "I don't want trouble, but it's here if you figure on making it."

Rubbing his stomach and left cheek, Royce edged across the floor to halt at Coxin's side. Cold, angry, savage eyes glared at Dusty. Then the hard-case became aware that a change was apparently taking place in the appearance of their would-be victim. No longer did he seem small or insignificant. Somehow he gave the impression of possessing the size and heft to tower over them both.

Shocked by the amazing metamorphosis, the hard-cases exchanged startled and nervous glances.

"Take him!" Coxin yelped and grabbed for the butt of his holstered revolver.

Hearing his companion's words, Royce also commenced his draw. The speed and determination with which they acted left Dusty no alternative. Bullies they might be, but either possessed sufficient skill and speed to prevent him from dealing with them by other means than the use of his revolvers.

Crossing so fast that the watching Stagge could barely follow their movements, Dusty's fingers closed about the bone handles of the matched Army Colts. The guns left leather as if possessed by wills of their own. All in an incredibly swift motion, the barrels turned outward, the triggers were carried to the rear by Dusty's forefingers and his thumbs drew the hammers to full cock. Then flame lashed from the muzzles and the twin detonations merged as one single sound.

Struck in the chest while his gun was just clearing its holster's lip, Coxin pitched backward. At almost the same instant, a .44 bullet ripped into the center of Royce's forehead. He twirled around once, collided with the front of the bar and tumbled face-first to the floor.

Shocked motionless by what he had just seen, Stagge

began to push back his chair. Hearing its legs scrape on the floor, Dusty swung the barrel of his right hand Colt in the gambler's direction. With the muzzle pointing directly at the center of his vest, Stagge halted his movements.

"I don't know how you fit in this," Dusty warned. "So just sit again and put your hands flat on the tab—"

Snarling out his agonized, wordless fury, Coxin supported his weight on the bar. Despite suffering from a mortal wound, he lifted his revolver in Dusty's direction. His pain-creased eyes flickered at Stagge and his mouth opened as if to ask for assistance in dealing with the man who had shot him.

"Look out, cowboy!" Stagge bellowed, swiveling his head to stare at Coxin.

Dusty had already caught a hint of Coxin's movements from the corner of his eye. Even as Stagge began the warning, the small Texan had whipped around and dropped his right knee toward the floor. If Dusty had been a fraction of a second slower in assuming the kneeling position, he would have been killed. Coxin's gun blasted and its bullet hissed through the air above Dusty's head.

By the time Dusty's knee reached the floorboards, he was ready to deal with Coxin. The ambidextrous prowess developed as a child, to draw attention away from his lack of inches, served him well, as it had on other occasions. Although his right hand Colt still covered Stagge, the left moved almost as if of its own volition. Angling upwards, the revolver bellowed in reply to Coxin's challenge. The bullet entered the hard-case's open mouth as his head twitched toward Stagge. Ploughing on, the lead burst through Coxin's brain and sprawled him lifeless across Royce's body.

Half out of his chair, standing as if turned to stone, Stagge stared at the bodies by the bar. Feet thudded in the hall and voices were raised excitedly outside the building as people, attracted by the sound of the shots, ran toward it. Dragoon in hand, Colin darted into the room. Peet followed the Scot, but skidded to a halt and allowed his revolver's barrel to sag toward the floor. All doubts as to

Dusty's identity had left him and he stared in awe at the small Texan. Bringing up the rear at a slower pace, the de Brioudes halted at the door and looked between the two men.

"Are you all right, Dusty?" Colin asked.

"What happened, *Captain Fog*?" de Brioude said, leaving his wife in the hall and walking forward. He laid emphasis on the last two words as if wanting to make sure that there were no doubts about who they were dealing with.

"Cap'n Fog?" Stagge repeated, slumping back into his chair.

The gambler's eyes swung to the small Texan, then jerked in Peet's direction and received a confirmatory nod.

"I am sorry that we did not recognize you when we met, Captain Fog," de Brioude remarked as Stagge appeared to be on the verge of making some comment to the hunter. "If we had, this would not have happened. But why should those men want to attack you?"

"A man like Cap'n Fog's made a heap of enemies, Arnaud," Stagge pointed out. "Could be they're two of 'em."

"I don't recall having seen either of them before," Dusty answered. "Anyways, I'm obliged for the warning, mister."

"It was all I'd time to do," the gambler replied.

Béatrice had been studying the scene in the barroom with a casual, detached interest. Hearing voices and footsteps drawing near to the front doors, a sudden change came over her. Leaning against the wall, she took on an attitude of distress that contrasted vividly with her previous behavior.

Several men and women, all dressed in what would probably be their best clothes, appeared at the doors. Taking the lead, a big, buxom woman entered. There was an air of standing no nonsense about her as she stalked toward the barroom. Close on her heels was a short, leathery old timer. He looked uncomfortable in his old suit and having the neck of his shirt fastened did not appear to be a normal state of affairs. For all that, he moved with quick, alert determination.

"What happened, ma'am?" the old timer inquired, increasing his pace and reaching the Vicomtesse ahead of the woman.

"Th—the—there has—been—a shooting!" Béatrice answered brokenly, bosom heaving with emotion.

"Land-sakes!" the big woman intoned, showing concern as she went to Béatrice. "And it happened afore you, your ladyship?"

"N—No!" the Vicomtesse sniffed. "I was in the dining room when it happened."

"Best take her back there, Annie," suggested the old timer and looked at the other people in the hall. "You folks stay put until I've seed what's coming off."

Although the other new arrivals belonged to the committee which had organized the reception for the de Brioudes and were the town's most influential citizens, they obeyed the request. Hovering in the main entrance, they talked among themselves in quiet, heated tones.

"Come on, your ladyship," Mrs. Annie Logan, owner of the hotel, said and led Béatrice back to the dining room. "Lord's a-mercy! That this should've happened today of all days. Not that it often happens. Fact being, we've never had a shooting here afore."

Still explaining that Kerrville was normally a most peaceful town, Mrs. Logan disappeared from the hall with Béatrice. Watching them go, the other citizens muttered threats against whoever had done the shooting if it should drive away the visitors. After a glance at the speakers, the old man went into the barroom. Keen eyes darted around, taking in the whole scene, then came to rest on Dusty.

"Cap'n Fog, ain't it?"

"It is," Dusty confirmed.

"Thought so," the old timer grunted. "I mind seeing you in Fort Sawyer when you, *Cabrito* and you, warn't it, young feller?" His gaze returned briefly to Colin but he continued without waiting for an answer, "went after the

Flores boys. Must admit I was a mite surprised when I heard who you was, Cap'n, you being—name's Ned Franklin, I'm town constable.[1] What come off here?"

"Those two fellers picked a fuss with me as soon as I walked in," Dusty explained, showing no annoyance at the implication behind Franklin's unfinished comment. Few people could reconcile him with the legendary Dusty Fog at first sight. "I tried to end it without shooting, but they started to draw on me."

"Anybody else see it?" Franklin inquired. "Which I don't doubt—"

"You have to ask," Dusty said and indicated Stagge. "This gent was here from the start."

"It was like Cap'n Fog told you," Stagge replied. "Those two fellers came in earlier, asking the Vicomte for work. He hired them and fixed it so they could wait in the barroom until after the reception. I figured they'd got a mean look and come in to sort of keep an eye on them. Arnaud, the Vicomte, allowed I should make sure they stayed out of trouble. It all happened so fast. Cap'n Fog had hardly reached the bar before they started picking fuss with him."

"You know 'em, Cap'n?" Franklin drawled.

"I've never seen them before today," Dusty stated. "Way they acted, I'd say they was on the prod and looking for somebody to take out their meanness on."

"You was here with 'em for a spell, Mr. Nerton," Franklin remarked. "Still, they wasn't likely to make fuss for a friend of their new boss."

"It's not likely they would," Stagge agreed. "Look, I'm tolerable sorry that I couldn't stop it—"

"Nobody blames you, Mr. Nerton," Dusty assured him.

"Nope, they don't," Franklin went on. "Well, gents, I reckon we'd best go into the dining room and talk things out. I'll have them two fellers moved to the undertaker's right now."

[1] Older Texans tended to use the term "constable" rather than "marshal."

"How long've they been around town?" Dusty
inquired.

"I ain't seed 'em afore," the old timer declared. "Which
means not more'n a day or so."

While answering Dusty's question, Franklin was
ushering the other men from the room. In the hall, the
various influential citizens stopped their muttering.
Stepping forward, the owner of the livery barn demanded
to be told who had been responsible for the shooting. A
low, menacing mutter rose from the people at the doors,
but died away as Franklin indicated Dusty.

"Couple of hard-cases on the prod picked a fuss with
Captain Dusty Fog here, Henry," Franklin explained.

"Cap'n Fog—!" echoed the owner of the barn. "*You're*
Captain Fog?"

"I am," Dusty admitted.

"Which it's right lucky they picked on him," Franklin
continued. "'Cording to the Count's *amigo* here, they was
looking for trouble and might've started on somebody
less able to take care of his-self."

Allowing a few seconds for his point to sink home,
Franklin led the way to the dining room. Colin noticed a
change come over the crowd. Much of their open hostility
had gone. They still talked among themselves, but in a
subdued and worried manner. At the door, Franklin
stood aside to let the other participants enter. He then
asked the undertaker, always a prominent member of a
range-country community, to attend to the bodies and
requested that Henry set up a hearing on the killings in his
capacity as Kerrville's justice-of-the-peace.

On entering the dining room, Dusty found Béatrice
seated at the table with the lace cloth. Standing
protectively alongside the Vicomtesse, Mrs. Logan glared
indignantly at the men.

"Whoever made that trouble—!" the buxom woman
began grimly.

"*Cap'n Fog* here didn't have no choice but to start
shooting, Annie," Franklin protested, indicating the
small Texan.

Chopping off her tirade, Mrs. Logan stared hard at

Dusty. She had noticed the definite manner in which Franklin had named him and understood what it meant. If that insignificant cowhand was Captain Dusty Fog, he belonged to one of the most powerful and influential factions in Texas. More than that. Rumor claimed him to be Ole Devil Hardin's favorite nephew. So he could not be abused or mean-mouthed, even if doing it might win favor from the de Brioudes. Wanting to change the subject, the hotel's owner swung her eyes to Béatrice and found a good way of doing it.

"Your necklace!" Mrs. Logan shrieked, pointing. "It's gone!"

Up fluttered Béatrice's hands toward her neck and she stared at Stagge in such a pointed manner that she drew the other occupants of the room's attention to him. Seeing the interest and even suspicion that the words had aroused, he seemed disconcerted for a moment. Then he dipped his right hand into his jacket pocket and started to draw out a diamond necklace.

"I've got it, Mrs. Logan," Stagge explained. "The catch broke and the Vicomtesse asked me to take it around town and see if I could get it fixed." As the end of the necklace emerged, it brought out a wad of ten dollar bills which fell to the floor. All eyes followed the money as it dropped, then lifted to Stagge's face. He bent and gathered it up, saying, "The Vicomte wanted me to buy some things for him while I was out."

"That is correct," confirmed de Brioude. "But we thought we had better leave doing it until after we were sure the two men meant no mischief."

Satisfied with the explanation, Franklin brought the hearing to order. Watching and listening to the old timer, Dusty felt sure that he knew his business. Despite Franklin's proficiency as a peace officer, little could be learned about the two dead men. According to Henry, the pair had arrived soon after Tam Breda had left with the posse, paid cash to stable their horses and had slept in his hay loft. Questioned about his connection with the pair, Peet declared that they had met him on the street and asked if he thought that his boss would hire them. Against

his better judgment, he had brought them to see de
Brioude. Out of the kindness of his heart, the Vicomte had
offered to employ them and arranged with Mrs.
Logan—who had arrived to make sure that none of the
other citizens were jumping the gun to meet the
visitors—to let them wait in the barroom. Stagge stated
that Dusty had been blameless of starting the fight and
had only drawn when it was forced on him.

Wanting to get the reception started, Henry had
exonerated Dusty. The hearing closed with a verdict that
a couple of bullying troublemakers had picked on the
wrong man for a victim and received no more than they
deserved. Franklin promised that he would try to learn all
he could about the pair.

Declining an invitation to attend the reception, Dusty
and Colin accompanied Franklin to the livery barn. De
Brioude had not concluded any deal with the Scot, but
promised he would visit the Schells' camp and do so. A
search of the dead men's property yielded no clue as to
their identity or reason for being in town. So Dusty and
Colin made ready to start their return journey.

"You're not saying much, Dusty," Colin remarked
after they had covered about two miles in near silence.

"I'm thinking some, though," the small Texan replied,
but did not mention the nature of his thoughts.

What if the whole affair had been a plot to have Colin
killed and obtain Mogollon for the de Brioudes?

Highly unlikely on the face of it, yet there had been
aspects which did not sit right with Dusty. Take "Nerton"
for starters. According to what Franklin said on the way
to the barn, the gambler had become friendly with de
Brioude in a card game and been invited on the hunting
expedition. "Nerton" fitted the general description of the
hired killer who had been circumvented by Tam Breda in
Fort Sawyer, as had the two hard-cases.

That could be pure coincidence, for Mark's description
had not been too detailed. No matter who he might be, the
de Brioudes trusted "Nerton" sufficiently to give him a
valuable necklace and a wad of cash money. They had

produced a convincing reason for doing so, but there might be another explanation.

What if they had planned to separate Colin from the companion they had believed to be an unimportant cowhand. Then when the Scot had heard the fight or shooting from the barroom, he would dash in and could be killed "in self-defence." Before independent witnesses arrived, "Nerton" would have placed the money and necklace on Colin's person and sworn it had been paid by the de Brioudes for Mogollon.

"But why the necklace?" Dusty asked himself and came up with a possible answer. "Colin said he'd told the de Brioudes why he wanted Mogollon. So they'd claim to have thrown it in as boot to help make up for her for losing the horse. That'd make them look nice folks come the hearing. Hell! It's *loco*. Even if the de Brioudes reckoned they could get away with it, 'Nerton'd' know that Tam Breda wouldn't let them no matter what the hearing decided."

Dusty kept his theory to himself. If it should prove true, the situation would require the most delicate handling. Going by various important citizens' reactions to the incident, the de Brioudes had made themselves very popular in Kerrville. For one reason or another, these same citizens would need a lot of convincing before they believed the couple capable of participating in such a murderous plot.

CHAPTER TWELVE

Never too amiable or easy tempered, Béatrice de Brioude was in a bitter mood as she rode along the narrow trail which led from Kerrville to the Renfrew ranch house. Her husband, Peet and Stagge knew the signs and waited to see which of them would be the victim of her anger. After spending the afternoon pretending to enjoy the reception, she wanted to lash out at somebody.

"I'll have my necklace back now," the Vicomtesse suddenly announced, thrusting out her left hand at Stagge. "And you can return Arnaud's money."

"Sure," the hired killer replied, returning the items calmly. "You could've had them back sooner, only that'd've made a lie of the story we had to tell because *you* let those folks know I'd got 'em."

"And what difference would it have made if those yokels had known we lied?" Béatrice demanded. "Or are you as frightened of them as you are of getting that horse for me?"

"I'm not frightened," Stagge growled. "But I'm not *loco* either. Way things went today, you've got the folks in Kerrville eating out of your hand."

"What do I care about that?" the Vicomtesse snorted.

"If you'd listen to Hubie," de Brioude interrupted, "you'd know why you should care. As he says, if there is trouble when we take the horse, we want the people of the town on our side."

"It would seem that, despite his recommendations, our protector suffers from a *very* strong sense of caution," Béatrice mocked.

"It's kept me alive," Stagge pointed out. "Libby Schell's got ten *mesteneros*, that Scotch feller, Dusty Fog, the Ysabel Kid and that big blond jasper who sided Tam Breda in Sawyer backing her. If you want me to lock horns against that bunch, I figure on having plenty of guns with me. Weasel's not back with them yet and even after they come, I want the folks in Kerrville with us."

Just as Peet had suspected, the de Brioudes had refused to let his failure lessen their determination to obtain Mogollon. Called in for advice, Stagge had insisted that they need more men before making hostile moves against Libby Schell's party. Although infatuated by Béatrice, Lieutenant Lebel would not permit his soldiers to be used for illicit purposes. With that in mind, Stagge had sent his third man to collect reinforcements from a small town where hard-cases of various kinds could usually be found. In addition to awaiting Weasel's return, Stagge had suggested that the de Brioudes should try to ingratiate themselves with the citizens of Kerr County.

The chance to do so had presented itself sooner than any of them could have hoped for. Reports of a large Mexican *bandido* gang marauding to the south had reached Kerrville. At Stagge's instigation on hearing the news from Peet, de Brioude had offered the services of his military escort to Tam Breda. In need of extra fire-power, for he had not yet organized his police detachment—and being unaware of Stagge's crowd working for the Vicomte—Breda had been only too willing to accept. The "magnanimous" action, taken with hints that they might be settling and bringing money into the county, had endeared the de Brioudes to the citizens. Sending Lebel off with Breda had also removed from the immediate vicinity two men who would have objected to the methods Stagge envisaged using to make the Schells part with Mogollon. Although she knew the plan, Béatrice still wanted to work out her spite.

"Are you so afraid of some—greasers, don't you call them?—and four boys that you need an army to help you?"

"Schell's greasers'd fight the devil for her. Nobody with

sense'd sell them or that Scotch feller short. Much less the Ysabel Kid. Them's have mostly wound up too dead to wish they hadn't. That big blond jasper's no slouch with his guns—and I saw just how good Dusty Fog is at first hand."

"You can't blame me for that!" Peet protested, sensing that Stagge was trying to turn the blame for the fiasco in Kerrville on to him. "I'd always heard Dusty Fog was as big as a house. He looked like two cents' worth of nothing; warn't even riding that big paint he's been using since the end of the War."

"I *knew* there was something about him as soon as I laid eyes on him," de Brioude insisted. "But the plan had been made—"

"Talking about that," Stagge interrupted. "Let's get that bill-of-sale burned right now. If it got into the wrong hands—"

"Caution *again*, Hubie?" Béatrice purred.

"Listen, *lady*!" Stagge spat back, showing anger for the first time. "You don't have any notion of what kind of folks you're fooling with. They're not dull-witted yokels. Even old Franklin's smart enough to start thinking things and coming up with the right answers if he should lay hands on that damned paper. Sure, Royce and Coxin haven't been seen with us around this way. But they were in Fort Sawyer. Give Franklin, Breda and Dusty Fog that much of a head start and they might want to know other things."

"Such as?" asked de Brioude.

"Why a French count and his wife'd have a feller like me trailing along," the killer replied, and read from the de Brioudes' expressions that he had scored a point. "They'll start thinking about that feller in Fort Sawyer being French—"

"There was no need for you to go after him," de Brioude objected sullenly.

"We all know that—now," Stagge answered. "Arguing about whose idea doing it was won't get us any place. The thing is that you want Mogollon—"

"And you had a so-clever idea to get it this afternoon,"

Béatrice mocked. "All we had to do was lure them to the hotel and send the cowhand into the barroom where your men would goad him into drawing a gun and shoot him, then kill Farquharson when he came to investigate."

"It would've worked if that short-growed son-of-a-bitch had been what he looked instead of Dusty Fog," Stagge declared. "Anyways, it cost me more than it did you. I lost two good men. I even had to warn Fog when it looked like Coxin was going to ask me for help. Fog'd got the upper hand by then. There was no other way."

"You didn't know he was Dusty Fog either, when we come to tell you that him and the Scotch feller was coming," Peet pointed out, determined to exculpate himself. "Or if you did, you never let on about it while we was watching 'em go by through the window."

"Nobody's blaming you, Abe," de Brioude said soothingly. "Here you are, Hubie."

A bitter, challenging sneer twisted at Stagge's lips. Instead of speaking, he took the sheet of paper offered by the de Brioude and glanced at its message.

"I, the under-signed, have this day sold one chestnut stallion called Mogollon to the Vicomte de Brioude for the sum of two hundred and fifty dollars and, as boot for the deal have been given one diamond necklace by the Vicomtesse de Brioude as a wedding present for my fiancée. The sale being witnessed by Abel Peet."

Perhaps an Eastern lawyer might have quibbled as to the document's legality, but Stagge felt certain that it would have been accepted by the influential citizens of Kerrville in their eagerness to please the de Brioudes. He also concluded that the sooner such a damning piece of evidence was destroyed, the safer he would feel. Producing and lighting a match, he set fire to the paper. When it was reduced to ashes, he discarded the remains with a sense of relief.

Dusty Fog had come close to the truth in his theorizing. The whole incident had been a plot to murder Colin and gain possession of Mogollon. Before any witnesses could reach the barroom, Stagge was to have placed the money and necklace in the Scot's sporran. Then the de Brioudes were to have claimed that Colin had sold Mogollon to them, been paid, but left the dining room and was killed before he had signed the bill-of-sale.

"*We* may not blame you," Béatrice continued. "But *I* would like to know when, if ever, you mean to get Mogollon for me."

"As soon as Weasel comes back with enough men to give us a better than fair chance of doing it," Stagge promised.

Although she gave a cold sniff, Béatrice let the matter drop. Determined to have revenge upon Libby Schell and Mark Counter, it had been the Vicomtesse who insisted that Kerr County would make the best starting point for their hunting expedition. Nothing had happened since her arrival to make her change her mind. During the journey, she had decided that Stagge was the man best suited to help her settle her score with Libby and Mark. Lebel had too many notions of honor to take part in her schemes. While Peet possessed no such scruples, he lacked the intelligence to be of more than a minor use. So that left Stagge. Possibly the fact that the killer had Laura along increased Béatrice's desire to make use of him. Being much alike in their attitudes toward members of the opposite sex, there had been some friction between the two women. Béatrice had contrived to have Laura left at the camp so as to be free to develop her relationship with Stagge. So far the opportunity had not arisen.

"What are the hunting chances around here, Abe?" Béatrice inquired after a short period of silence.

"Not too bad," Peet answered, relieved to notice that her temper appeared to have changed for the better.

"Then why don't you and Arnaud go and shoot some—camp meat, isn't it?" the Vicomtesse suggested. "Hubie and I can find the way to the camp easily enough."

"Why not, Abe?" de Brioude agreed. "Come along. If the new men have arrived, we will need the meat. We'll join you at the camp, my love."

Earlier in his association with the de Brioudes, Peet had been surprised by the Vicomte's behavior. Although he must have known of his wife's indiscretions, he had made no attempt to curb them, nor showed anger over them. Peet did not care for the idea of leaving Stagge with Béatrice, but consoled himself with the thought that they would soon be at the Renfrew place where Laura was waiting.

"Do you think that we are foolish to try to take Mogollon, Hubie?" Béatrice asked as she and Stagge continued to follow the trail and the other two swung off at an angle.

"I'd say that depends on what you're figuring on doing with him after you've got him," replied the killer.

"Arnaud plans to make money by racing him."

"He'll have to go up North to do it. There's not enough money in Texas, or the rest of the South, to make racing him worth what it'll cost you to get him."

"So you believe we are wasting time and money doing it?"

"Not if you play your cards right," Stagge told her.

"How do you mean?" Béatrice wanted to know.

"Get that hoss, by all means," Stagge explained. "Only don't bother about roaming around racing it for nickel and dimes. Stay on here, take over that ranch and make it your home."

"Why should we do that?"

"Because I've got a hunch you can't go back to France and that you're a gal who wants as much out of life as she can lay her hands on."

"Go on," Béatrice offered, neither confirming nor denying his summation.

"You've already got most folks in Kerrville eating out of your hand," Stagge continued. "That spread's not too big, but you've got all you need to make it grow. Land's cheap enough down here. You'd soon own more than you ever did in France—and I'll be on hand to take care of whoever's following you if he comes."

Eyeing her companion in a speculative manner,

Béatrice let almost half a mile drop behind them before she spoke. All the time, her eyes darted around and took in the rolling, grass-covered scenery.

"You think we can do as you say, Hubie?" she finally asked.

"I *know we* can," Stagge assured her. "You—and Arnaud—have got the money. I can hire men and know how to make sure you get all the land you need."

"And what will you get out of it?"

"The job as segundo—at first."

"And later?"

"Way Arnaud treats you," Stagge replied, "I don't reckon you'd be grieving or mourning happen he wasn't around."

"That's something to think about," Béatrice purred, easing her horse closer so that she rubbed legs with the killer. "I'll think; once I've seen if *this* plan works out better than your last."

Riding on in the same intimate manner, Stagge continued to elaborate on his scheme. He claimed that the fiasco in Kerrville could be turned to their advantage by establishing that one of the Schells' friends had already gunned down two of the de Brioudes' hired hands. It would be a point remembered by the townspeople once trouble started. Nor, according to Stagge, would anybody be willing to face up to an outfit which had defeated Libby Schell's *mesteneros* and Dusty Fog's OD Connected contingent. So buying more land would become easier.

Despite the glowing picture Stagge painted, there was one aspect that he did not mention. Although it had turned out that there was no reason for him to try to kill the man in Fort Sawyer, Stagge could neither forget nor forgive Breda's intervention. Stagge's shoulder had been sore for hours and he hated to think of the humiliation stemming from Breda having him held in the town's jail. So, like Béatrice, he had come to Kerr County in search of vengeance.

The plot Stagge had made that afternoon should have set him on the way to achieving his ends. Even as he had reassured de Brioude that there could be no legal come-back, he had known that, no matter what the citizens' hearing found on the two killings, Breda would insist on conducting an independent investigation. Once that had happened Stagge had believed that he could arrange Breda's death in such a way that the peace officer appeared to be the aggressor.

The scheme had come to nothing due to Dusty Fog, but Stagge had no intention of giving up his revenge. Backed by the de Brioudes' money, he felt sure that he could not only take it but also pave his way to a fortune.

Any hope of furthering his ideas regarding Béatrice ended as they came into sight of the ranch's buildings. Sturdy, well-constructed and erected with defense in mind, the house, barn and combined bunk-and-cook-shack formed an "n" shape. Two pole corrals faced the open end of the "n." Although showing signs of neglect, the spread's headquarters could easily be brought into a most satisfactory condition. So far the de Brioudes' party had carried out only such repairs as were necessary for a brief period of occupation.

Thinking about the repairs and alterations he would make if his employers accepted his plan, Stagge saw men emerge from the cookshack. Three he identified immediately as their cook, wrangler and Peet's skinner. If their general appearance meant anything, the other five had been sent by Weasel. In fact, on going closer, Stagge discovered that he knew the quintet. Slouching forward with hands thumb-hooked into revolver-and-knife-ladened belts, the newcomers devoted most of their attention to gazing hungrily at Béatrice.

"Howdy, Hubie," greeted the lank, bewhiskered, buckskin clad man in the lead, dragging his eyes reluctantly from the Vicomtesse.

"Howdy, Buck-Eye," Stagge responded. "Hi there, Roarke, Clum, Walde, Orell. It's good to see you all again."

In the order named, the last four men were respectively: medium-sized and stocky; big and heavily built; tall, lean and bearded; and scrawny, middle-sized, with a face even a mother would have trouble loving. The first two wore buckskins. Walde sported cowhand clothes and Orell had on a filthy Confederate States infantry uniform which had lost its military buttons and insignia. While Béatrice normally enjoyed being the center of male attention, she found the newcomers' scrutiny a little disconcerting. She had seen similar lascivious expressions when other men had heard of her easy-going nature in sexual matters.

"We met up with the Weasel," Clum remarked, devouring Béatrice with a lust-filled stare. "He told us to come on over's you're hiring men, Hubie."

"Where's he now?" Stagge demanded.

"Gone on up to the Fork to see who-all's in town," Clum answered.

"What's it all about anyways, Hubie?" asked Orell. "Laura's been hitting the Taos Lightning 'n' couldn't tell us nothing."

"Least-wise, nothing's we could go repeating afore a for-real lady," Walde went on, looking pointedly at Béatrice. "She's sleeping it off up to the house right now."

A low hiss of anger broke from Béatrice as she listened to the men's comments. Up to that point, she had been blaming Weasel for describing her character in an uncomplimentary—if fairly true—manner. From what she had just heard, the source of their information was much closer at hand.

"We'll tell you about it when the boss comes back," Stagge promised and dismounted. "Ramon! Come and tend to the horses."

"*Si, senor,*" answered the wrangler, advancing.

"Hold it back there, boys!" Stagge ordered as the five men made as if to move in Béatrice's direction. "The Vicomtesse rides good enough to get off without needing help."

Saying the words, Stagge opened his jacket and placed himself between Béatrice and the newcomers. With his right hand pointed toward the butt of the concealed revolver, there was a challenge and a threat in his attitude. Stagge knew the kind of men he was dealing with and that he must assert his domination over them from the start. So he seized on their behavior toward the Vicomtesse, as the excuse for a showdown.

Slowly Stagge's eyes turned from face to face, remaining on each until its owner looked away. Béatrice could sense the tension, but ignored it. At that moment she was too furious at Laura to worry about what the men were doing. If she had possessed more knowledge of the situation, she would have had a greater awareness of the danger.

However, the newcomers had no collective reason to go up against Stagge. Nor had any single individual the necessary guts to take on the cold-eyed killer. All realized that they had not seen Royce and Coxin since their arrival and suspected that the two men could be close by, ready to back their boss's play should it be necessary. So the men put aside their individual desires to see if Laura had been telling the truth about the foreign woman.

"Have you boys fed yet?" Stagge inquired in a more friendly manner, satisfied that he had made his point for the time being.

"Was just set to when we heard you coming," Buck-Eye replied.

"Go to it then," offered Stagge. "You'll find you've not had the ride for nothing when the Vicomte comes home."

Leaving the wrangler to attend to their horses, Béatrice and Stagge went into the house. Buck-Eye and his companions watched the door close, then returned to the cook-shack, discussing the Vicomtesse's possible relationship with the killer. One thing on which the newcomers agreed, Stagge had given them a "hands off" warning which he would be wise to take.

On leaving the ranch, the Renfrew family had taken most of their furniture. So the de Brioudes had been forced to make do with their own camp equipment and items salvaged by their escort. Expecting to move on after a week or so, they had taken little trouble in refitting the buildings. The main house's front room had only a rickety table, six folding camp-chairs and blankets hung at the windows to preserve the occupants' privacy. Three doors in the rear wall led to the bedrooms and kitchen which were just as scantily furnished.

"That woman you brought must go!" Béatrice shrilled at Stagge as they stood in the front room. "She's been talking to those men about me!"

Hinges creaked and a disheveled, bleary-eyed Laura came from the bedroom allocated to her and Stagge. Barefooted and wearing only a loosely fastened, flimsy robe, she swayed forward to confront Béatrice and the killer.

"So what if I did?" Laura challenged, teetering to a halt on wide spread feet. "I only said you was a gal who'd sleep with anything in pants—"

Leaping by Stagge as he moved toward Laura, Béatrice hurled up her left leg with a speed that took the other two by surprise. Powerful muscles propelled the toe of the riding boot between Laura's thighs. White-hot torment burst through the brunette. Clutching at the stricken area, she folded over and collapsed on to her side. Laura's whole being wanted to scream aloud, but the unexpected agony had robbed her lungs of air and she could make no sound.

Almost as soon as Laura struck the floor, Béatrice had lowered her left leg and kicked with the right. Teeth splintered and blood gushed from the brunette's mouth as the boot struck her face. The impact rolled Laura on to her back, the robe trailing open. Spitting out a string of French gutter-oaths, the Vicomtesse stamped first one foot then the other into Laura's naked body and features.

Amazed by the animal speed and fury of Béatrice's attack, Stagge allowed six stamping kicks to descend on Laura before he made a move. By that time, the brunette's face was a mass of gore and blood was dribbling from the nipple of her left breast. Striding forward, Stagge caught Béatrice's right arm and jerked her away from the supine, motionless woman. Around whipped his free arm to slap the Vicomtesse's face. For a moment he thought that the blow would bring her rage on to him. Then sanity returned and Béatrice relaxed.

"Get her away from me, Hubie!" Béatrice ordered, reverting to English and studying her victim without displaying compassion. "Throw her out and tell her not to come back."

"And have her go straight to town and tell the law what she knows?" Stagge growled. "Like hell. And she could be too useful to kill, before you say it. Go to your room. Buck-Eye always totes a sleeping potion with him. I'll use that to keep her quiet until we decide what to do with her."

CHAPTER THIRTEEN

Seeing a thin column of smoke rising from a clump of post oaks, Mark Counter turned his horse in that direction. He was on his way back to the Schells' camp after an abortive visit to Kerrville, but decided to see who had made the fire among the trees. Jeanie and Colin planned to make a *corrida* on four *manadas* which had been located to the northwest of the *Caracol de Santa Bárbara*, so Mark intended to ask whoever he found to stay clear of that area until it was completed.

On Dusty and Colin returning from Kerrville the previous evening, they had told the others about their visit. In view of Libby's annoyance over hearing that the de Brioudes apparently intended to purchase the Renfrew ranch, Dusty had kept quiet about his theory. Taking Mark and the Kid aside later, he had confided to them. Even with Dusty's more detailed description to guide him, Mark had been unable to claim definitely that "Nerton" and the two hard-cases were the same he had seen in Fort Sawyer. Agreeing with Dusty that they must act warily and be sure of their facts, Mark had suggested that he should visit Kerrville in the morning and examine the bodies. They had been buried by the time he arrived, so there was no chance of him identifying them. As Tam Breda was still away with the posse, Mark had learned the latest developments and was headed back to tell Dusty what had happened. Probably the small Texan would find other means of checking out his theory.

Passing through the post oaks, Mark approached a small clearing. Two wiry, smallish horses stood hobbled on the bank of a narrow stream which flowed across the open space. Going by the fact that they still had on their saddles and hackamores, Mark concluded that their owners did not intend to make an extended stay in the area. From the horses, he turned his eyes toward the fire. A coffeepot steamed on the flames and two buckskin-clad men stood facing him. They held tin cups in their left hands, the right fingers close to their holstered revolvers. That did not surprise Mark, for they were merely taking an ordinary precaution. Mark had made no attempt to conceal his presence while riding up, but he had expected whoever he found to be wary.

"Howdy, gents," Mark called, halting the bloodbay and resting both hands on its saddlehorn to display his pacific intentions. "Can I come ahead?"

"Feel free," answered the taller of the pair. "Seth 'n' me've got coffee to spare. Light 'n' take a cup."

"Thanks," Mark drawled, setting the horse moving. "I could sure use one."

Watching the blond giant swing from his saddle and lead the big stallion towards the stream, Seth Roarke spoke quietly to his companion.

"Reckon it's that Counter jasper the Countess wants to see so bad, Buck-Eye?"

"Ain't likely there's two that size around," the lanky man answered in no louder tones. "Anyways, his guns, hoss and gear'll bring in a good price if he's not. Fill your cup, *pronto*."

Obeying swiftly, Roarke held the filled cup to his companion. Showing an equal speed, Buck-Eye had produced a small buckskin pouch from a pocket built inside his shirt. While Mark was attending to the stallion's needs, his back to the fire, Buck-Eye tipped powder from the pouch into the cup. Agitating the contents, Roarke caused all traces of the addition to disappear from the liquid. With the stallion's thirst quenched, Mark set it free to graze and joined the men by the fire.

"You working hereabouts, friend?" Roarke asked, holding out the cup.

"I'm helping the Schells catch mustangs for my

spread," Mark replied, for the question had not exceeded the bounds of frontier etiquette.

"They wouldn't be hiring, would they?" Buck-Eye inquired, watching the big blond accept the cup. "Seth 'n' me could use work real bad."

Mark took a sip at the coffee before answering. While crossing the clearing, he had studied the pair. They looked a little different from the usual run of drifters and might be hunters or mustangers. Maybe they possessed a tough, unprepossessing appearance, but he could hardly hold that against them. Certainly they seemed amiable enough and Libby could use some extra help with the next *corrida*.

"Why not ride on over and ask Mrs. Schell?" Mark suggested and looked at the black liquid in the cup.

"Coffee all right?" Buck-Eye asked. "We're nigh on out of sugar, so it won't be over sweet."

"It'll do," Mark answered, putting the fluid's slightly bitter taste down to the shortage of sugar. "You boys been mustanging?"

"We've had to turn our hands to more'n one thing since the War," Buck-Eye said. "Ain't nothing paying worth a damn these days."

After that the conversation followed general lines about conditions in Texas. Mark saw nothing suspicious and the men gave no hint of their interest in his consumption of the coffee. Emptying the cup, he returned it to Roarke.

"If you gents want to come along," Mark said, "I'll take you to see Mrs. Schell. Can't promise anything, mind, but there'll be a meal in it for you any way it goes."

Starting to walk toward his horse, Mark felt a sudden wave of dizziness strike him. For a moment he tried to clear his head by shaking it. Then his legs buckled under him and he found himself falling. Through the mists which seemed to be swirling about his head, he heard the soft thud of the men's moccasin-covered feet coming toward him. Their voices appeared to be a long way off.

"How long'll it make him sleep, Buck-Eye?"

"Until near on midnight. We'll have him to her afore then."

"Why do you reckon she's so set on getting him?"

Everything went black for Mark before he heard the reply.

"Now why'd *you* think she wants him, Seth?" Buck-Eye grinned, stirring Mark's unconscious, giant frame with the toes of his left moccasin. "'Specially after what Laura told us about Mrs. Count."

"Which I bet ole Laura's wishing she'd not said nothing," Roarke commented. "Whoever rough-handled her sure did one hell of a job of it."

"Yeah," grunted Buck-Eye. "Anyways, Mrs. Count's offering a good price to whoever fetches Counter in on the hoof. And Hubie Stagge won't let none of us get close enough to find out if Laura done had a mistake 'n' told the truth for once."

"You had a right smart notion, coming down this way," Roarke enthused. "We made us a good catch."

"Don't go figuring I'm all magical-like," Buck-Eye warned. "Coming here was a whole heap safer'n going some place that we might've run across *Cabrito*. Douse the fire and let's load him up 'n' head back to the ranch."

When de Brioude had returned the previous evening, he had given his blessing to Béatrice's and Stagge's suggestion of settling permanently in Kerr County. Interviewing the new arrivals, the Vicomte, with Stagge's backing, had told them what would be required of them. With money in such short supply throughout Texas, Buck-Eye and the others had agreed to work for the de Brioudes. Of the opposition, only Dusty Fog and the Ysabel Kid—especially the latter—had attained sufficient prominence to cause the hard-cases any anxiety. Even that was stilled by de Brioude's assurance that they would not be asked to clash head-on with the Schells' faction until enough men had arrived to give them numerical superiority. Pointing out that the five must earn their keep, Stagge had suggested that they should go on the scout around the county. If the chance to do so in safety arose, they were to reduce the enemy's fighting strength.

Buck-Eye in particular had reservations about the soundness of Stagge's proposals and had shared them with Roarke. Killing Schell employees could easily spark off an open confrontation before Weasel brought in reinforcements. Apart from that, no man with an ounce of sound common sense would deliberately set out to hunt down the Ysabel Kid. Few who tried it lived to confess their folly. So, once clear of the ranch and other hard-cases, Buck-Eye and Roarke had made for an area in which they would be unlikely to meet up with memebers of Libby Schell's party.

Despite their precautions, they had come into contact with a member of the opposition. Resting in the clearing, they had seen a rider approaching through the trees and realized what an advantage fate had thrown their way.

With the introductory meeting ended, a poker game had commenced. Taking her chance while the others were occupied, Béatrice had managed to contact each of the five in private. Nothing romantic had ensued. Instead she had offered every man a hundred dollars if he could capture and bring Mark Counter to her. Recognizing the blond giant from Béatrice's description, Buck-Eye and Roarke had decided to make the most of their opportunity. Clearly their visitor suspected nothing and Buck-Eye's "sleeping potion" had reduced him to helpless unconsciousness. All that remained for them to do was deliver Counter to the Vicomtesse and collect their reward.

The first part of that proved easy enough. Physically strong and skilled horse-handlers, they experienced no difficulty in lifting Mark or draping him belly-down across the bloodbay's saddle. Then they gave thought to what they should do next. In addition to wishing to avoid sharing the loot—Mark's horse, saddle, weapons and other valuables—with their companions, they remembered that the Vicomtesse wanted the delivery to be made in secret. Which meant that they would have to arrive at the ranch after dark. According to Béatrice, her husband could be expected to spend most nights playing cards with the other men at the buckhouse. So Buck-Eye and Roarke believed that they could carry out her stipulations with no great danger of detection.

Making their plans, but not forgetting to keep a careful watch all around, the two men led Mark's stallion and left the shelter of the post oaks. They saw nobody during the journey to the ranch. Night had fallen by the time they arrived, so they brought the horses to a halt at the rear of the corrals. Telling Roarke to watch over their victim, Buck-Eye first visited the cook-shack. Everything was as Béatrice had predicted, for de Brioude was sitting in the poker game with Stagge and the other men.

Slipping away from the window undetected, Buck-Eye crossed to and circled around the house. He knocked gently on the side door and heard soft footsteps approach it on the inside. Gun in hand, Béatrice opened the door a couple of inches and peeped out. Cold suspicion showed on her face, but died as she heard his news. Hard and tough though he might be, Buck-Eye felt uneasy at the glow of hatred which replaced the Vicomtesse's previous expression.

"Bring him here!" Béatrice hissed eagerly.

"Sure, ma'am," the lanky man replied. "We'll put up his hoss—"

"Leave it saddled and ready," Béatrice corrected. "There will be another hundred dollars in it for you if you do as I ask with *le beau* Counter after I've finished with him."

"You've hired a man," Buck-Eye promised. "Wait a whiles and I'll fetch him to you."

"Bring some pieces of rope with you," Béatrice hissed. "Hurry."

Gliding away silently, Buck-Eye rejoined Roarke. On hearing of the Vicomtesse's offer and requirements, Roarke agreed to help. Producing several rawhide thongs from his saddlebags, Buck-Eye thrust them into his pocket. Then the two men removed Mark from the bloodbay's back and carried him to the side entrance of the house. At Buck-Eye's knock, Béatrice opened the door. Ignoring the two men's bug-eyed scrutiny, for she

wore her diaphanous robe over more scanty underclothing than either had ever seen, the Vicomtesse
allowed them to carry their burden into the front room.
Closing the door, she found them awaiting her instructions.

"Put him on his back on the table," Béatrice
commanded. "You have brought the ropes?"

"Sure," grunted Buck-Eye as he and Roarke carried
out the order. Mark lay motionless, arms and legs
dangling over the table's edges. "You want for us to
hawg-tie him for you?"

"No," answered Béatrice. "Remove his gunbelt and put
it on that chair." She saw their startled glances and
continued, "I may want to do some shooting with his
guns, you see."

While they did not see, the men raised no objections.
Buck-Eye lifted Mark's torso and held it up until Roarke
had unbuckled and slid free the gunbelt.

"Anything else, ma'am?" Roarke asked, hanging the
belt on the back of a chair.

"Just the ropes," Béatrice replied. "Oh yes! Make sure
that nobody comes near here until I send for you."

"What if it's your husband?" Buck-Eye queried.

"He's the last you need worry about," the Vicomtesse
stated. "How can I get to you when I want you?"

"Seth'll be with the hosses at the corral, ma'am,"
Buck-Eye suggested. "And I'll stop at the bunk-house."

With the arrangements completed, the men took their
departure. Dropping the door's bar into place, Béatrice
made sure that all the blanket drapes were fully closed.
Satisfied that nobody could see into the room, she slunk
like a great cat toward the table.

Something cold and wet splashed on to Mark's head
and jolted through the haze which filled it. He opened his
eyes and looked at a lamp suspended from the ceiling of a
cabin. Hard planks, which shook and creaked a little,
supported him and he became aware of the uncomfortable position in which he was lying. Shaking his head, he
tried to sit up. Then he realized why his arms had been

drawn above his head. Bent at the elbows, their wrists were fastened to the legs of a table. The same applied to his feet. Raising his head, he discovered that his shirt had been removed. In fact, unless he guessed incorrectly, he was completely naked. Growling a curse, he tried to tear himself free.

"It's no use, *chéri*," purred a sultry feminine voice he recognized.

Twisting his neck, Mark saw the Vicomtesse approaching. Her bare body was quivering with lust and passion. In her eyes flamed a light as cold and chilling as the steel of the spear-pointed knife she carried. Up and down whipped her right hand, spiking the blade into the table close to his face. Then she leaned over, her nipples brushing against his chest. Digging her left fingers into his hair, she held his head still and lowered her face. Hot lips crushed against Mark's and her tongue tried to thrust its way into his mouth. At the same time, her right hand explored his body like a spider crawling about on its web.

"So! You don't kiss back!" Béatrice spat, jerking erect when her embrace produced no response. "This is the second time you have spurned me. But you will make love to me now, or I swear you will never make love again. By the time I'm finished, you'll be good for nothing but a eunuch in a harem. If you know what that is."

To emphasize her point, she fondled the area of his body that would be affected by such an operation. A lusty, vigorous young man, Mark could not prevent an involuntary reaction to the treatment. Whispering incoherently, Béatrice swung herself from the floor and crouched astride the big Texan. Louder groaned the ancient timbers of the table at the increased burden placed on it.

Sweat flowed freely from Mark's pores, soaking his bonds. By the time Béatrice lifted herself into a kneeling position above him, he could feel the thongs loosening. Rawhide might be strong and practically unbreakable, but it stretched when wet. Taking advantage of the slight slackening, Mark twisted his right hand until his fingers gripped the table's leg to which it had been fastened.

"Wasn't that better than your fat old woman?" Béatrice gasped, panting from her exertions.

"She even kissed better than you," Mark replied.

"Kissed!" the Vicomtesse spat and acted as Mark had hoped she might.

Throwing herself forward, she pressed her face to Mark's. Instantly he gave a tremendous outward tug with his right arm and ankle. Already straining almost to the breaking point, the affected legs tore free from the rest of the table. Tipping over to the right, Béatrice was tumbled from Mark's body. As the edge of the table struck the floor, the knife slipped free and bounced a few feet across the boards.

Winded by the fall, Béatrice sprawled on her back. Giving her no time to recover, Mark rolled on to her. He could feel her voluptuous body writhe in a desperate attempt to escape. Ignoring the pain caused by her teeth biting at his chest, he started to rock back and forward on top of her. Savagely he ground his two hundred and eighteen pound frame to crush her against the floor. At last her struggles ended and she fainted. Mark continued his pressure for a few more seconds to make sure that she was not bluffing. Satisfied on that score, he rolled from her. Collecting the knife, he contrived to set himself free. Béatrice lay where he had left her, moaning a little as she dragged air into her lungs.

"The next gal's asks me to sleep with her, I'll sure as hell do it," Mark mused as he stood up and looked around. "I'd hate to have her go to this much trouble if I don't."

With that, he donned the long-john underpants, socks, shirt and Levi's removed by the Vicomtesse before she had fastened him to the table. His gunbelt came next. Strapping it on, he checked that the Colts had not been unloaded. Having taken the precaution, he drew on his boots. While collecting his Stetson, he noticed that the Vicomtesse had rolled on to her stomach and was forcing herself on to her hands and knees. Distorted with frustrated rage, her face looked old and haggard as she turned to glare at him. Then she started to scream. Shriek after shriek burst from her, shattering the silence of the night.

"That does it!" Mark growled as shouts rang out from beyond the building.

Starting toward the door on the side away from the shouts, Mark slapped the Stetson on to his head. Still screeching fit to wake the dead, Béatrice hurled herself at him. She came with teeth bared and hands crooked like talons, raging like a madwoman.

Although Mark had never seen or heard of football, he reacted as if he had played the game all his life. Thrusting out his left arm, he placed the flat of his palm on her face. For an instant her rage-strengthened impetus caused even that mighty limb to bend. He felt her fingernails clawing through the material of his shirt's sleeve. Straightening his arm, he flung the Vicomtesse backward. Coliding with the wall, all the air once against burst from her lungs. Her screams ended as her feet slipped forward and she slid, glassy-eyed and mouth working soundlessly, to the floor.

Giving the naked woman no further attention, Mark flipped up the bar and tore open the door. As he sprang into the open, he saw a man emerge from a building that, by its shape, would be the backhouse. The supposition was supported by the fact that the man was holding up his pants with his left hand. His right gripped a revolver.

"Hey!" yelled the man, bringing up the gun and firing—to miss.

Mark's right hand dipped and closed on the ivory handle of his off-side Colt. Out it came in less than a second and roared from waist level. Struck in the chest by the blond giant's bullet, the man pitched backward into the small cabin.

Already men had reached the opposite side of the house; Mark could hear one of them pounding on its door as he fired. Without wasting further time, the big blond started to run toward where he detected the presence of horses. Moving fast and swerving, he made a poor target for the figures who appeared at the far end of the building.

Guns crashed and lead made its eerie sound as it winged by the Texan. In the corrals, disturbed by the shooting, horses snorted and milled around. Not only *inside*, Mark observed as he drew nearer. Three animals backed and tugged at the reins which secured them to the rails on the outside at the rear of the enclosures. There was sufficient light from the stars for Mark to recognize his bloodbay. Forgetting his original intention of opening a corral's gate and escaping on one of the horses from it, Mark directed his feet toward the stallion.

Moving swiftly along the curving side of the corral, hidden from the men by its occupants' restless milling, Mark kept on the alert. One of the approaching horses suddenly veered away from the railings, snorting in alarm. Instantly Mark hurled himself sideways. Thrusting himself erect from where he had been crouching in partial concealment, Roarke cut loose with his revolver in the blond giant's direction. Mark missed death by little more than an inch, but he did not let that distract him. Swinging his Colt's barrel parallel to the ground, Mark fired three times as fast as he could thumb-cock the hammer and control the recoil. Fanning ahead of him, two of the bullets missed their target. The third took Roarke in the head as he attempted to correct his aim. Spun around by the impact, the man involuntarily discharged his weapon but its load flew harmlessly across the range.

Striding on as Roarke went down, Mark reached his objective. Swiftly he set free Buck-Eye's and Roarke's horses. Going to his own mount, he unfastened his reins. Although the men from the buildings were running toward him, Mark took time to ensure that his saddle's girths had not been loosened. Finding all to be satisfactory, he swung into the saddle. Flattening himself forward along the bloodbay's neck, he turned it and started it moving. A few shots followed him, but none came close and he knew that there could be no pursuit until de Brioude's hired hands had saddled their horses. Catching the spooked horses and doing so was likely to be a lengthy business.

After covering almost a mile, Mark brought his horse to a halt. He listened, but could not hear any sounds of following riders. Pausing to try to get his bearings, he set off in what he believed to be the direction of the Schell's camp.

CHAPTER FOURTEEN

"Soldiers coming, Dusty," warned the Ysabel Kid, bringing his horse to a sliding halt by the Schell's camp fire. "Around a dozen of 'em, I'd say."

The time was shortly after noon and the mustanging party had returned from making a successful *corrida*. Instead of the rest and relaxation they had expected, Jeanie and the men had discovered the reason why Mark had failed to return the previous night.

Being unfamiliar with the country he had to traverse and still feeling the effects of the ordeal, Mark had not reached the camp before dawn. By the time he had arrived, he found only Libby and the cook present. When Libby had learned what had happened, she wanted to recall her people and head for the Renfrew place. Knowing that the *corrida* would be started before they could reach Jeanie, Mark had suggested that they should wait until the work was finished.

Discussing the situation, Libby and Mark had concluded that the de Brioudes lacked the men to attempt reprisals. Nor did it seem likely that the Vicomte would report the matter to the law. "Constable" Franklin might be long in the tooth, but he was a fair and smart peace officer. There would be too many aspects which the de Brioudes could not explain to his satisfaction for them to want Franklin involved. Even if the Vicomte should call Franklin in, relying on his popularity to gain the town's support, Mark knew that Dusty and the others would be in camp before a posse could arrive. The big blond also felt sure that the power of Ole Devil Hardin's name, backed by his friends' guns, would ensure him a fair hearing. So he had insisted on taking no action, a decision which met with Dusty's approval when the small Texan was told of it.

Not that Dusty had wasted time in congratulations. While the kidnapping of Mark might have been carried out at the Vicomtesse's instigation, if her husband did intend to obtain Mogollon by violent means she had presented him with an excuse to attack the Schells' party. So Dusty had swiftly made arrangements for their defense. Accompanied by five of the *mesteneros*, Jeanie had been sent to guard the captured mustangs in the *Caracol de Santa Bárbara*. Telling the Kid to make a scout in the direction of the Renfrew ranch, Dusty had given orders to the remainder of his companions. Before half an hour had passed, the Kid returned at a gallop with news.

"Soldiers, huh?" Dusty drawled. "From the de Brioudes, do you reckon?"

"Down that way at least," the Kid replied. "There's a feller in buckskins with 'em, could be a scout."

"How long before they get here, happen they're coming?"

"Fifteen, twenty minutes at the soonest. They're riding slow and watchful, like they was expecting trouble."

"Colin!" Dusty snapped, blessing his decision to keep the Scot at the camp instead of sending him with Jeanie. "Take Mogollon and head as fast as you can for Kerrville. If de Brioude's escort've come back, you'll find Tam Breda there. If he's not, see Franklin and tell him what's happened. Only watch how you go in town."

"Trust me for that," Colin replied and headed for the corral at a sprint.

"This's what I want the rest of you to do," Dusty went on as the Scot made a record time at transferring his saddle to the chestnut stallion's back.

Riding in front of his twelve men, Lieutenant Lebel gripped his reins so savagely that his knuckles showed white. Tight-lipped and fighting to prevent his anger from showing, he searched the land ahead for the first sight of the Schell's camp.

Having helped Tam Breda to deal with the *bandidos* earlier than he had expected, Lebel had hurried to rejoin the de Brioudes. Before he had agreed to assist the peace officer, Béatrice had intimated that she would be waiting gratefully when he came back. Instead he had found her suffering from a brutal assault. Guided by Peet, the besotted young officer had set out immediately to arrest the man responsible, or, if Mark Counter resisted, to kill him without mercy.

At Lebel's side, Peet was also scouring the range. Sent to town that morning to gather help, the hunter had covered less than half the distance when he had seen the soldiers. So he had turned his horse and ridden swiftly to let de Brioude know the military escort was returning. The news had caused a change in the Vicomte's and Stagge's plans. Instead of attacking the Schells with their own men and such of Kerrville's citizens who would join them, they would let Lebel do it for them. Completely infatuated by Béatrice, the young lieutenant had needed little convincing that a great wrong had been done to her. Told the same pack of lies, Lebel's enlisted men had shown an equal desire to avenge the Vicomtesse. There had only been one part of the plan which failed to appeal to Peet, he was ordered to guide the patrol to the camp on Wolf Creek.

When the camp came into view, Peet slackened his horse's pace and let the soldiers go by him. Absorbed in his cold-eyed scrutiny of the area, Lebel did not notice that Peet was falling behind. After the last man had passed him, the hunter reined his horse to a halt. Selecting a clump of buffalo-berry bushes, he made his way there and concealed himself behind them. From that position, crouching in his saddle to reduce the chance of being seen, he watched the patrol ride by.

Oblivious of the hunter's desertion, Lebel examined the Schell's camp. Two wagons stood sideways-on to his party. Between them, Libby Schell, Mark Counter and a big, plump Mexican cook were gathering around a fire. At first Lebel felt puzzled as he looked at the trio. None of them showed more than ordinary, casual interest in the approaching soldiers. Lebel decided that their lack of concern was understandable. It was unlikely that Counter had told his companions how he spent the previous night. So the woman and her cook saw nothing unusual in the patrol's visit. Maybe the big blond believed that he had escaped unrecognized from his crime and so had nothing to fear from Lebel's arrival.

Fifty yards from the wagons, Lebel ordered the patrol to halt, dismount and draw their carbines. Leaving the horses ground-hitched, the men formed into two ranks. Spitting into the grass at his feet, Sergeant Heaps opened his saddle's left side pouch. From it he drew a set of leg-irons and a pair of handcuffs.

"I forgot to give these back to Breda," Heaps commented as Lebel darted an inquiring glace at him. "Could be they'll come in useful."

"They will!" the officer confirmed grimly, and led his men forward.

"Howdy, young feller," Libby said, placing hands on hips and eyeing the lieutenant coldly. "There's some's'd say it's polite to wait until you're asked to do it, but we've got to mind you're Yankees. So come up to *my* fire and rest yourselves."

Annoyed by the implied criticism of his manners, Lebel brought his escort to a stop farther from the fire than he had originally intended.

"I'm here on official business, ma'am!" he announced stiffly.

"Such as?" challenged Libby.

"I'm going to arrest that man," Lebel answered, indicating Mark.

"What for?" Libby asked, doing as Dusty had told her.

Deciding that the woman would be more amenable to reason if he treated her with frankness, Lebel sucked in a deep breath. His upbringing and training had instilled firm ideas of what should or should not be mentioned when addressing a member of the gentle sex. So he needed a moment to prepare himself for the disclosure.

"Last night Counter raided the de Brioudes' camp, raped the Vicomtesse and killed two men while he was escaping," Lebel explained, eyes glowing hatred at the blond giant. "Put the handcuffs and leg-irons on him, Sergeant."

"Yo!" Heaps barked, jingling the instruments of restraint in his hands. A wolfish leer twisted at his lips, for he doubted if the big Texan would permit such an indignity.

Taken with the lieutenant's words, the sergeant's too obvious eagerness to obey ripped like a knife into Mark. Instead of continuing to follow Dusty's instructions, the big blond tensed like a cougar preparing to spring.

"The only way you'll do it is after I'm dead," Mark warned, hands hovering the butts of his Army Colts. "And I'm not ready to die just yet."

About to accept Mark's defiance as an excuse to start shooting, Sergeant Heaps identified a sinister double clicking noise which came to his ears. It was the sound made by a Henry repeating rifle being charged and brought to full cock—and the soldiers carried nothing but single-shot Sharps carbines.

Swiveling their heads in the direction of the sound, the cavalrymen saw the Ysabel Kid bound from the rear of the right side wagon. He landed with a cat-like grace, facing them. No longer did the Kid seem young or innocent, but created an impression of savage, deadly menace as he gripped the new model "Henry" ready for instant use. Like Mark, the Kid sensed that Lebel's and Heaps's hostility went beyond the needs of their duty. Never a respecter of authority and having little liking for the Union Army, the dark youngster forgot the part he had been told to play.

"Happen you're fixing to put them things on Mark, blue-belly," the Kid said in a voice almost angelically mild and gentle. "Just come ahead and try it."

Silently cursing his *amigos'* response, although he

realized what had caused them to disregard his orders, Dusty sprang from concealment over the box of the other wagon. He came with empty hands, but there was that air of command about him which had so often made men forget his actual height.

"That's enough, Mark, Lon!" Dusty snapped. "And you keep a tight hold on your men, mister!"

Much to his annoyance, Lebel found himself stiffening into a parade ground brace. He had heard that tone of voice before when a tough, capable officer possessing rank higher than his own addressed him. Angrily he halted his training-induced reaction. The speaker was not an officer of the Union Army—empowered by Acts of Congress and the military disciplinary code to command obedience—but a *big* Texas cowhand. An officer with superior rank to lieutenant he might have been in the Confederate States Army, tough and capable he most certainly was. However, neither qualification gave him the right to issue orders to ɪst Lieutenant Charles Lebel.

"Do you duty, serg—!" Lebel ordered, secure in the knowledge that numerical superiority favored his patrol.

"Take a look around, *mister*," Dusty interrupted, right hand lifting. "Then maybe you'll stop trying something you'll have cause to regret."

Swiftly leaving the rear of the wagon from which Dusty had emerged, Félix Machado carried a shotgun in his left hand and gripped the wrist of a Sharps carbine's butt with his right. Tossing the shotgun to Libby, who caught it deftly, he transferred the fingers of his liberated hand to the carbine's foregrip. Reaching behind his back, the cook produced a Dragoon Colt. Cradling a Mississippi rifle ready to be brought to his shoulder, Bernardo rose into view on the box of the right side wagon. Nor did the increase in the Schell faction's numbers end there. Following the movements of Dusty's pointing forefinger, the patrol saw three more *mesteneros* armed with rifles rise from cover. Whoever had selected the trio's positions clearly knew his business. They were ideally placed to inflict the maximum damage to any enemy occupying the ground on which the soldiers stood.

"So you're protecting the murd—!" Lebel blazed.

"Way I've always heard it, *mister*," Dusty cut in, "a man's innocent until somebody proves him guilty."

Again the small Texan had prevented words being spoken that could have set guns roaring. Fearing Ole Devil Hardin's potential strength in the political field, Davis's corrupt Reconstruction Administration would be only too willing to turn to their advantage the news that OD Connected men had killed members of the Union Army. So Dusty had made plans to reduce the danger of it happening. Everything, from Libby's comment on Lebel's lack of etiquette to the positioning of the men, had been made with that end in mind. What Dusty had not taken into consideration was the threat of using handcuffs and leg-irons on Mark. Once that had been made and answered, the whole situation rested precariously on a knife-edge. The slightest wrong move might easily prove fatal.

Watching from behind the buffalo-berry bushes, Peet scowled and cursed under his breath. Instead of charging up with guns blasting, that hawg-stupid luff had set his men afoot and led them straight into a trap. Studying the disposition of Libby Schell's party, Peet grudgingly admitted that they had the soldiers over a barrel. If Lebel tried to arrest Counter, he stood a better than even chance of losing most of his patrol—which would not be a bad thing as far as de Brioude's scheme was concerned. The trouble being that Lebel stood like he recognized the danger and intended to avoid making hostile moves. He might even listen to Counter's side of the story and, knowing the Vicomtesse, decide to check into it. What the son-of-a-bitch needed was something to trigger him off and start him throwing lead.

At which point, Peet saw a difficulty in supplying the trigger. Riding into town that morning had not seemed a task which required that he tote along his heavy Sharps rifle. Nor had he collected it when told to guide Lebel to the Schell's camp, as he did not intend to become involved in the expected fighting. All he had on him was his holstered Leech & Rigdon Navy revolver and a Kaddo tomahawk strapped to the other side of his gunbelt. The latter weapon would be of no use, but the revolver might serve his needs.

All too well Peet could imagine the sense of tension which had built up at the camp. Every man's nerves would be taut as they concentrated on snapping into motion at the first hint of danger. If he started firing the revolver even from such a distance, nobody would wait to learn who did it, or why. At the first shot, all would suspect the worst and take instant action for their own "protection." Grinning viciously, the hunter started to draw his handgun.

Holding Mogollon to a fast, mile-devouring canter, Colin Farquharson turned a bend in the valley he was following and found himself confronted by three riders. One wore travel-stained range clothes and looked like a Texan. The second hailed from east of the Mississippi River if his outfit was anything to go by. There could be no doubting the last man's occupation. He had on the uniform of a major in the United States cavalry. Debating what action he should take, Colin saw the Texan's face take on a warm smile.

"*Cárn na cuimhne!*" the stocky Westerner whooped.

Instantly Colin's misgivings ended. Although he had not met Tam Breda, the Clan Farquharson's slogan identified his cousin. Riding to meet the trio, Colin clasped Breda's hand.

"I'm pleased to mee—!" Breda began.

"There's trouble at the camp, Tam!" Colin interrupted. "If we hurry, we may stop it."

"Let's go then!" Breda snapped, knowing that only a desperate situation would cause Colin to be so abrupt and unsociable.

Turning Mogollon, Colin accompanied the three men. While riding at good speed, he darted glances at them. He liked everything he saw of his kinsman, figuring that Breda would qualify as a forty-four caliber man. Swarthily handsome, the civilian had a sturdy build and his clothes came in the middle price range. There was an air of authority about him, despite his lack of visible weapons. Tall, lean and middle-aged, the major belonged to the regiment which occupied the post at Fort Sawyer. Going by his expression, he was on a mission of importance and did not relish being diverted by a side issue.

On coming into sight of the camp, Colin let out a sigh of relief. Despite the hostile attitudes of the figures ahead, no trouble had started. With Tam Breda and the major present, it was unlikely to do so.

"We're in ti—!" Colin ejaculated.

"Look over there!" Breda barked, pointing. "Behind them buffalo-berry bushes."

Following the direction indicated, Colin saw Peet drawing the revolver and guessed the hunter's intentions. Maybe Colin had not been long in Texas, but he could imagine what would happen if Peet started shooting.

"Get down there!" Colin yelled. "I'll stop him!"

In fact the young Scot had already achieved his part of the affair. Hearing the shouted words, Peet swung his head around. At the sight of Colin setting out toward him, the hunter forgot all about helping the de Brioudes. Loyalty had never been a matter of great importance to Peet. He had been willing to start a fight between the two groups, but drew the line at risking his own life.

Turning his brown gelding, Peet nudged it into motion with his heels. A glance over his shoulder warned him that he must drive the animal to the limits of its endurance if he hoped to escape. Wanting to increase his control of the horse, he attempted to replace the Leech & Rigdon in its holster. No fast-draw exponent, preferring to use his rifle or tomahawk depending on circumstances, his gun-rig did not make for easy withdrawal or return of his revolver. While Peet managed to thrust the handgun partially into its holster, he found himself compelled to take his hand from it so as to grip the reins. Ignoring the gun's insecure fit, he concentrated on urging more speed from his mount.

Behind Peet, Colin allowed Mogollon to build up the long, raking stride which had so often carried it to safety before mustangers. Rested all morning and warmed up by the work it had already carried out, the huge stallion seemed to skim over the ground at an ever-increasing rate. Although Colin had prevented Peet from starting the fight, he had no wish to see the man escape. No doubt Peet could explain some of the mysterious events which had taken place since the de Brioudes had first made their offer to buy Mogollon. So Colin allowed the horse to run and hoped to catch up with the fleeing hunter.

Looking to the rear, Peet found that the distance between himself and Colin had lessened. Trained for hunting, the gelding still could not hope to out-run the great stallion. Too often in the past, Mogollon's speed and endurance had been the means of retaining its freedom. Peet could see how the *manadero* had avoided capture for so many years.

Two miles fell behind Peet, with Mogollon slowly but surely eating away at the distance separating them. Between the hunter's knees, the lathered gelding was showing signs of distress. Neither Peet's flailing with the reins nor heel-kicks could make it run faster. In fact, its pace was weakening. Twisting in his saddle, Peet could detect no slackening in the chestnut stallion's racing gait. It ran as if powered by a machine rather than flesh and blood.

Ahead of the hunter, the land fell away into a valley. He had not tried to go back the way he had come, but cut off across country in the hope of eluding his pursuer. So he did not know the nature of the slope beyond the rim. He found out soon enough. Down plunged the incline, steep and dotted with rocks. At the sight of the terrain, the gelding screamed and tried to turn. Rearing on its hind feet, it fought against the reins and Peet's efforts to guide it forward. Down went the horse, pitching its rider from the saddle. Only luck saved Peet from injury. He landed rolling, the revolver falling from his holster, and managed to halt himself as he tipped over the edge.

One glance told Peet that he could not remount the gelding before Colin arrived. However, another avenue of escape presented itself. No man could ride a horse faster than a walk down such a slope. Nor did it seem likely that a dude in a skirt could match a hardened frontiersman if he gave chase on foot. So Peet shoved himself erect and started to descend. Becoming aware of his empty holster, he spat a curse. There was no time to go back. In fact, agile as he was, Peet found that he had all his work cut out to retain his footing and prevent himself from tumbling the rest of the way.

Colin had benefited from seeing how Peet's gelding responded to the land beyond the rim. Slowing Mogollon, he brought it to a halt instead of trying to follow the hunter over. Taking one look at the slope, Colin reached the conclusion Peet had expected. Mogollon was far too valuable to be endangered by descending into the valley. However, the hunter had been way out with his second opinion.

Dismounting and allowing the reins to dangle, ground-hitching Mogollon, Colin plunged over the ridge. Before him lay the sort of terrain over which he had roamed and played most of his life. Down went the Scot, keeping his footing with the ease of a bighorn ram on a mountain. Bounding from rock to bare ground, skimming over cracks and avoiding treacherous places, Colin made far greater speed than the man he pursued. In fact Peet had as little chance of leaving Colin behind as the gelding had had of out-running Mogollon.

Turning as he reached the floor of the valley, his attention attracted by falling stone which he had not dislodged, Peet received the shock of his life. That fancy-dressed dude was coming down the incline as if on level ground.

"God blast you!" Peet screeched, grabbing at his holster and finding it empty. From there, his hand flashed to and started to snatch the tomahawk from its sling. "I'll—"

The moment of forgetfulness ended the hunter's chances of escape.

"*Cárn na cuimhne!*" Colin bellowed and the valley's sides flung back the slogan in ringing echoes.

Thrusting himself from the rock on which he had landed, Colin hurled down at Peet. Before the tomahawk came clear of its retainer, they crashed together and went down. Prepared for the impact, Colin came out of it best. As they struck the ground, he had the upper position. Straddling the winded hunter's torso with his knees, Colin plucked out and tossed aside the tomahawk. With his other hand, the Scot slipped the *sgian dubh* from its sheath in the top of his stocking.

"Give up, or you're dead!" Colin threatened, pricking the point of the little knife under Peet's chin.

"Do—don't do it!" croaked the hunter. "I know when I'm licked."

"Get up!" Colin ordered, leaping to his feet and clear of the man. "You've got some explaining to do to Dusty Fog—or the Ysabel Kid."

CHAPTER FIFTEEN

"Well, Mr. Lebel," Major Aarhorte said coldly. "What's this all about?"

"I came to make an arrest, sir—" the lieutenant answered.

"And, from what I saw when we rode up, your behavior had almost provoked a gun battle."

"After the Vicomtesse de Brioude told us what had happened—"

"You and your men came rushing over here, without checking on her allegations, determined to take Mr. Counter back dead or alive," Aarhorte interrupted, before Lebel could explain that he and his escort had been filled with rightous indignation by her story. "You didn't even wait to hear his side of the affair before Heaps started waving those leg-irons."

"Well, sir—!" Lebel spluttered, trying to find an adequate explanation for what he now saw to have been a badly bungled piece of work.

The arrival of Breda, Aarhorte and the civilian had ended any immediate danger of gunplay. To show her good faith, Libby had called in her *mesteneros* and told them to go to join Jeanie. Dusty had dispatched the Kid to see if Colin needed help to capture the hunter. Sending Lebel's patrol to their horses, Aarhorte had requested an explanation. Recognizing the major from his stay in Fort Sawyer, Dusty had not hesitated to lay the full facts before him. There being sufficient food available, Libby had offered to feed the soldiers. While the enlisted men ate a good meal, Lebel had found himself called to his troop's commanding officer and faced with a demand for an explanation.

"No harm's been done here, Major," Breda said, after Lebel had listened to Mark's version of the incident. "And it's sure not a thing you'd think of a for-real lady doing."

"I can hardly believe she'd do such a thing!" Lebel croaked.

"Nothing Béatrice Argile did would surprise me, *m'sieur*," commented the civilian, entering the conversation for the first time.

"Béatrice Argile?" Lebel repeated. "Who's she?"

"You know her as the Vicomtesse de Brioude," the man explained.

"This is Inspector Maurice Fontaine of the—the—" Breda began.

"*Sûrété Nationale*," supplied the man. "The French police, *m'sieur*."

"The inspector's come over from Paris, France, to arrest the de Brioudes," Breda continued.

"Why?" Lebel yelped.

"Because they are not the de Brioudes," Fontaine explained. "They are Béatrice and Arnaud Argile and I've been on their trail for some time."

"How come?" Mark inquired. He stood with Libby, Dusty, Breda, Aarhorte and Lebel, listening to the French police officer, some distance from where Férnan fed the soldiers.

"They travel around Europe, taking employment as valet and maid," Fontaine replied. "From all accounts, they give satisfaction—until they rob their employers. In two cases we suspect that they went further than just robbing. And I am certain they did in another. It seems that they had to leave France hurriedly. Argile is an inveterate gambler and owed much money to a gambling syndicate, while his wife's indiscretions in love-making had caused the death of a prominent criminal's son. Fortune smiled on them, however. They were employed by the Vicomte de Brioude, who was bringing his wife for a hunting holiday in America."

"So they killed the count and countess and took their

places?" Breda guessed. "How'd you get on to them?"

"A word here, my friend, a rumor there. It led me to the de Brioude's mansion in the South of France. But when I arrived, I find that *M'sieur le Vicomte* and his wife had gone. Left one night, without a word to anybody, taking their maid and valet with them as arranged."

"Only they hadn't gone very far," Dusty guessed.

"We found their bodies in an old, disused well," Fontaine answered. "Further investigations showed that the Vicomte had drawn all his money and jewelery from his bank; it was collected by his valet, the afternoon before their boat sailed. Argile is an excellent forger. I discovered that the Vicomte and Vicomtesse alone took the boat, their papers being in order. So I was sent to arrest and bring them back. The man and woman who boarded the boat had been the Argiles. With their criminal associations, they had arranged for false documents."

"They also had some genuine letters of introduction from important folks in France," Aarhorte remarked. "Which's how come they arrived in Texas with orders from Washington that they was to have a military escort for as long as they needed it. Hell, it's happened often enough for us to take them as what they pretended to be."

"I'd say they didn't think a military escort was enough protection," Dusty commented. "That's why they had Stagge along. They figured either the law or some of their enemies'd find out where they'd gone and come after them."

"And that's what the fuss was about in the Grand Hotel," Breda growled. "When the Creole feller showed up there, Stagge's bunch took him for a Frenchman hunting the "de Brioudes" and tried to gun him down."

"Would this Argile *hombre* know how to find a feller like Stagge in a strange country?" Mark wanted to know.

"Probably he would," claimed Fontaine. "Most important criminals have contacts in other lands. Clearly the Argiles had, for they found and hired this man."

"Those fellers in Kerrville were Stagge and his bunch, then," Dusty said.

"Everything points that way," Breda agreed. "Looks like Stagge took my advice, Mark."

"How's that?" the blond asked.

"He's changed his way of working. Didn't have Laura nor the Weasel along," Breda replied.

"The man we call Nerton's wife's name is Laura," Lebel supplied.

"It's Stagge for sure," Dusty said. "What brought you out this way, Tam?"

"I'm going to arrest the 'de Brioudes,' so's the inspector can deport them."

"And you've come to have us ride in your posse?" Mark guessed.

"Sure," Breda admitted.

"Can't your soldiers take them for Tam, Major?" Libby asked.

"Well, ma'am," Aarhorte answered, looking embarrassed. "I've orders to leave the arrest to the civil authorities."

"Why?" Libby bristled.

"Could be the Yankee Army don't want it known they can't tell a genuine count and countess from a couple of owlhoots," Mark suggested with a grin.

"There may be something in that," Aarhorte snorted, then gave a shrug. "It's none of my doing. They're orders passed down from Washington, through the Commanding General. But if you can't manage, Tam—"

"I'll get by, John," Breda replied, guessing that the major intended to defy orders and offer the soldiers' services if necessary. "Can I count on your help, Cap'n Fog?"

"All with way," Dusty assured him.

"I'd've come here even if the Army could've helped, Libby," Breda remarked.

"How come?" the blonde wanted to know.

"One of the things a peace officer's wife has to do is handle female prisoners," the Scottish-Texan explained. "So I was hoping you'd come along and 'tend to that French gal for me."

"There's nothing I'd like better," Libby stated grimly,

then a smile creased her face. "That's the damnedest way of proposing to a gal I've ever heard of, Tam Breda. But you did it afore witnesses and my answer's 'yes.'"

Although the other men, including Breda, laughed, Inspector Fontaine looked grave and concerned.

"I beg you not to treat this matter lightly, *madame*," the Frenchman said. "Béatrice Argile is a vicious, desperate and dangerous woman."

"I'll mind it," Libby promised. "You can have as many of my *mesteneros* as you need, Tam."

"How many men we need depends on how many they've got," Dusty commented. "And on whether Colin caught that Peet *hombre*."

"I hadn't noticed he'd left us!" Lebel put in sullenly, having identified the hunter in the course of his explanation.

"You wouldn't've wanted a civilian along anyways, mister," Dusty consoled him. "Thing being, if Peet escapes and lets the de Brioudes know what's happened, they'll run for the border."

"Or stop and make a fight of it," Breda continued. "Depending on how many men they've got."

"Not counting my men," Lebel said as the others looked his way, "they had Nerton, his wife, Peet, a skinner, wrangler and cook. Mr. Counter killed the skinner last night."

"And another feller," Dusty reminded. "Who-all was he?"

"Some drifter who'd stopped by for the night," Lebel answered. "Or so Arn—the Vi—he told me."

"That'd maybe be one of the pair who caught me," Mark said. "Did he wear buckskins, mister?"

"Yes. He was a stocky, mean-looking man—" confirmed the lieutenant.

"Wasn't there a tall, lanky son-of-a-bitch wearing buckskins around?" Mark asked.

"Not that I saw," Lebel admitted.

"Hey!" Breda injected. "The Weasel's not at the ranch and wasn't staying in town 'cording to Ned Franklin. I'll bet he's been sent up to Grey Fork to hire some guns. Likely he met them two jaspers on the way and sent them to Stagge."

"Thing being," Dusty said. "Just how many men did he meet up with and send?"

Although Lebel could not supply the answer, Peet presented the required information when the Kid and Colin brought him to the camp. Having spent what seemed like several hours listening to the Kid describe his fate if he refused to give his full cooperation, the hunter was only too willing to do so.

In addition to telling his audience the number of men at de Brioude's disposal, Peet cleared up other matters. He confirmed Dusty's theory about the incident in the Logan Hotel. Then he explained that Weasel, Royce and Coxin had been left in Fort Sawyer for a few days to see if anybody came looking for the Vicomte. On their arrival in Kerr County, the trio had kept clear of the ranch house and camped at an old line cabin so that Lebel would not learn of their connection with the "de Brioudes." With Tam Breda away hunting the *bandidos*, the two hard-cases—near to mutiny through being deprived of company—had been allowed to go to town. Lastly, he said that the new men and their horses had hidden on the range while Lebel was at the ranch.

"You say this Laura's been beaten badly," Dusty remarked when Peet had finished "cooperating."

"Kicked 'n' stomped'd be closer to it, Cap'n," the hunter corrected.

"Is she still alive?"

"Was when I left. They've kept her locked in the storeroom at the back of the barn. She's drugged with Buck-Eye's sleeping-potion most of the time."

"Could be she'll give us some more answers to get even with them," Dusty told Breda, for there had been details upon which Peet could not supply information. "How many men'll you need?"

"You OD Connected boys, Dusty," Breda decided after a moment's thought. "The inspector'll be with us. I'll take Félix and Bernardo if I can, Libby."

"They're yours," Libby affirmed. "Will that be enough?"

"I reckon so," Breda replied.

"You didn't include me," Colin pointed out.

"Somebody has to stay here and tend to things, laddie," Breda answered. "And with Libby 'n' me along, the Clan Farquharson'll be well-enough represented."

"With you and old Mogollon catching this *pelado*, they'll not know we're coming," the Kid went on. "Happen they don't have any more men come in since he left, we'll be more than enough."

"To hell with orders!" Aarhorte suddenly growled, then directed a cold scowl at his subordinate. "You didn't hear me say that, did you, mister?"

"No, sir," Lebel answered. "Shall I tell the men to saddle up?"

"Yes," the major confirmed. "We'll be about half a mile behind you, Tam. And if we hear shooting, we'll join you fast."

A gentle tapping at the side door of the Renfrew house brought an indignant Béatrice Argile—alias the Vicomtesse de Brioude—from her bedroom. Closing and fastening a robe over the black tights which were her only garment, she stalked to the door.

"Who is it?"

"Buck-Eye. Open up. I've got something to tell Hubie."

"What makes you think he's—?" Béatrice began.

"Don't you fuss me none!" Buck-Eye's voice growled back. "He ain't at the card game, to the barn nor backhouse. Where the hell else would he be?"

"Who's there, Béa?" demanded Stagge from inside the room she had left.

"That Buck-Eye creat—" Béatrice spat back. Since assuming the Vicomtesse's identity, she had been accorded a respect which she had found vastly satisfying and come to expect. So she took exception to being addressed in such a manner by one of the hired help.

"Let him in!" Stagge snapped.

"Thanks," grunted the lean man when Béatrice opened the door. Slouching into the room, he sat down. "Could use a drink, gal. Walking allus gets me thirsted-up."

"A dri—?" Béatrice spluttered. "How dare you come—"

"Get him one!" ordered Stagge, coming from the bedroom still tucking his shirt's flap into his trousers and bare-footed. "What happened, Buck-Eye?"

"My hoss put his foot in a gopher hole 'bout five miles back," the man answered and looked pointedly at Béatrice. "I'm too thirsted to talk."

"Bring him that drink, damn it!" Stagge snarled. "Don't argue. This could be all our necks."

Startled by the vehemence and urgency in the killer's voice, Béatrice scuttled into the bedroom. She returned with a half-full bottle of brandy and a glass. Pouring a quantity of the amber liquid into the glass, she handed it to Buck-Eye and watched him swallow it at a gulp.

"Not bad," Buck-Eye commented. "Least-wise, it'll do 'stead of a real drink." Then, seeing Stagge's frown, he went on, "First off, Hubie, them soldiers ain't arrested nor shot Mark Counter."

"They haven't?" the killer growled.

"Nope. When I saw 'em, they was all sitting around Libby Schell's camp as sociable as borrowing neighbors at a wedding-feeding. Tam Breda's there along of some dude and a blue-belly officer. Way the luff of your'n was bowing 'n' bobbing to him, he's a captain at least. Which ain't all. Abe Peet's there with 'em."

"That dirty, double-dealing—!" Stagge snarled.

"You're doing him a wrongful, Hubie!" interrupted the lanky man. "Way things looked, I'd say he'd been took prisoner. Soon's I saw how things was going, I pulled out and headed back here."

"Is that all?" Béatrice snapped. "Why didn't you creep nearer and learn more?"

"'Cause they've got a young feller knowned as the Ysabel Kid with 'em," Buck-Eye explained with insolent patience as if addressing a foolish child. "Mrs. Count, you don't creep closer 'n' learn things when he's around—

'cepting maybe how it feels to get killed quick and painful."

"Are they coming here?" Stagge asked.

"Warn't when I left," Buck-Eye replied and looked at the bottle. "I was knocked silly for a spell when my hoss fell, Mrs. Count, 'n' need something to help clear my head."

"Give him another drink, Béa," Stagge instructed. "And when you've had it, Buck-Eye, get Roarke's horse and ride out about a mile. Stay there until you hear them coming, then come back and warn us."

"I'll get ole Seth's hoss right enough," Buck-Eye muttered after he had left the house. "But I sure's hell don't conclude to do the rest. If they come, *Cabrito*'ll be scouting ahead and I wants to live to see sun-up tomorrow."

"What was all that about?" Béatrice demanded.

"Just me being cautious and looking out for *your* interests," the killer replied. "As soon as Buck-Eye came out of hiding with the others, I sent him after Lebel. I figured it would be safer if he knew should anything go wrong."

"And something has gone wrong," Béatrice said bitterly.

"Just as far wrong as it could go," Stagge admitted. "With what Peet'll tell them, Breda, rot his guts, and Dusty Fog're smart enough to figure plenty out. They may even get around to figuring that you and Arnaud aren't what you claim to be."

"How did *you* know that?" Béatrice hissed, eyes flashing dangerously.

"Up to now, I only guessed it. There were little things pointed the way for me. Arnaud always acted more like a servant than a feller used to being served. And you sure took good care of your clothes and packed them tidy, for a gal who'd had a maid to wait on her all her life. Then there was how a real, genuine French Vicomte on his first visit to the United States knew the right folks to hire somebody like me."

"Go on!"

"I played along with you, watching and listening." Stagge continued. "Which I speak French pretty good—"

"You never told us about that!" Béatrice accused.

"I never put *all* my cards on the table," Stagge declared. "Not that you pair ever let out anything I could've used, I'll give you that. This Mogollon foolery gave me the chance I'd been looking for."

"How?" Béatrice asked.

"There wasn't much real hope of that notion about taking over Kerr County coming off," Stagge replied, satisfied that he was impressing her with his brilliance and intelligence. "And it got less when Arnaud would send Lebel to take Counter. That way, no matter how it came out, it wouldn't've ended there. Neither the Army nor Ole Devil Hardin would have let it."

"You didn't say anything like this to Arnaud," Béatrice said pensively.

"Why should I?" Stagge grinned. "Now *you* need *me* more than him."

"You seem sure of that."

"I am. Arnaud might be one slick he-coon around a big city, but he's lost out here. I can get you and all your money away and even fix it so that nobody from this country or France'll bother you again."

"Our enemies will never stop looking for me, even if they get Arnaud," Béatrice objected.

"They will," Stagge promised. "Because you and Arnaud will both be dead."

CHAPTER SIXTEEN

Backing in fright toward the bedroom's door, Béatrice opened her mouth to scream. Before she could make a sound, Stagge sprang to her. Scooping her into his arms, he kissed her hard.

"That's only what folks'll think," the killer said as he loosened his hold. "They're going to find things looking like Arnaud died trying to save you from a fire down at the barn."

"A fire—?"

"At the barn. I'll need your wedding ring and some of that jewelry you had on at the reception in Kerrville. Stuff folks'll recognize."

"I don't—" Béatrice began, then nodded vigorously. "The trinkets won't burn, but Laura's body will."

"That's using your head, Béa gal," Stagge praised. "I knew she'd be useful if we kept her alive. I'll fix it so that she's burned to a cinder, but leave Arnaud so that he won't be so bad marked up. That way everybody'll think how we want."

"And then what?" Béatrice inquired, nestling closer to Stagge.

"We'll head for the border with your wealth, you and me," the killer replied. "With that much money down there, we can live like a king and queen."

"And what of the men?"

"They'll be too busy fighting the fire to see us slip away. If we set loose all the horses, they can't follow us. It'll be dawn before anybody can find our trail and by then we'll be miles on our way."

"How do we get Arnaud to the barn?" Béatrice wanted to know.

"Easy," Stagge answered. "First off, we get everything ready; horses saddled, money and stuff on them. Then I'll go to the barn and fix Larua up. You fetch Arnaud from the game, make up some tale to get him to the barn."

"I could say that Abe Peet has come back and wants to speak to him in private—about you. That should do it. There's only one thing wrong."

"What?"

"If I go to Arnaud dressed for riding, he will be suspicious."

"Then have your clothes ready and go like you are," Stagge told her. "You've been to the bunkhouse dressed that ways before now. Once you've got him headed for the barn, come here and put your traveling clothes on."

"I must admit that you seem to think of everything, Hubie," Béatrice complimented and thrust her face to his. "If only we had time to finish—"

"We'll have all the time in the world after tonight," Stagge assured her.

"I can hardly wait," Béatrice purred and they started to make their preparations.

"I just don't figure it all," said the Ysabel Kid in a puzzled, almost aggrieved tone. "Don't those jaspers know *I'm* in Kerr County?"

"What's up, Lon?" Tam Breda inquired.

"There's not a single one solitary son-of-a-bitch out on guard," explained the Kid, having just rejoined his companions after making a thorough scout of the Renfrew property.

"You'd've expected them to have at least one out," Dusty commented. "Even without knowing *you* was in Kerr County."

"Maybe they don't know their little game's gone sour on them," Mark suggested. "Lebel allowed that he'd told them he'd take me straight to the Kerrville jail after he'd arrested me."

"They'd've expected Peet to come in and tell them

about it," Dusty objected. "Is anybody at the ranch, Lon?"

"I didn't look too close," admitted the Kid. "But there's some hard drinking 'n' a poker game in the bunkhouse."

"Who's in it?" Breda asked.

"That French *hombre*, a Mexican *pelado*, feller's might be their cook 'n' three hard-cases."

"Just them, Lon?"

"Nary a sign of anybody else, Dusty," stated the Kid, then slapped a hand against his thigh. "Hey though! I thought I heard a hoss moving off as I first come up. Maybe their guard up and lit a shuck out of it."

"It could be," Breda admitted. "Only that'd mean they know what's happened."

"Or only some of them do, Tam," Dusty corrected. "What if they had a feller watching, besides Peet? Then he came back, told what he'd seen and was sent out to stand guard. Only he allowed it'd be safer to make a Mexican stand-off."

"They'd not be drinking and poker playing if they knew what did come off at our camp," Mark protested. "Which could only mean somebody's playing all smart 'n' sneaky."

"One of 'em'd be that foreign gal for certain sure!" Libby put in. Wearing Levi's pants, a shirt-waist and moccasins, she had stood listening to the men.

"And the other's Stagge," Dusty guessed.

"I'll swear he's not in the bunkhouse," the Kid declared. "You boys told me what him 'n' the Count looked like, so I'd know one from t'other."

"Well!" Breda said. "Standing here whittle-whanging won't give us the answers. The folks who know 'em're waiting for us."

"How do we play it, Tam?" Mark inquired.

"We go 'round the back of the cookshack and surround it," Breda replied. "I'd sooner chance disturbing the horses than going into sight of the main house." The others muttered agreement and he continued, "Lon, you're the one to take the front. Whistle when you're there and all bust in at once. Libby, you'd best wait—"

"Stagge and the gal might get away unless they're taken at the same time as the others, Tam," Dusty warned. "Somebody should round them up."

"You're right," Breda admitted. "You and me'll do it, Libby."

"Your place is with the boys," Libby objected. "So why not leave Stagge and the foreign gal to Dusty 'n' me?"

"All right," Breda answered after a moment. "You're faster with a gun than me, Dusty, anyways. But don't take chances with Stagge. He's a killer all the way."

"I'll mind it," Dusty promised.

"We'll move out," Breda ordered. Letting the men set off, he caught Libby by an arm and swung her to face him. "You watch what you're doing, lassie."

"Count on it," the blonde replied and kissed him. "I've got too much waiting for me to take fool chances."

Knowing the lie of the land, Libby had suggested a route that would bring them to the ranch at the rear of the barn. In that way, they could reach the house or cookshack while keeping the other building between them and the horses in the corrals for as long as possible. They had around half a mile to cover, the Kid having decided that it would be unsafe to ride closer. Once again the dark youngster glided ahead, fading into the blackness as silently as a shadow. Before they had covered half of the distance, the Kid materialized before them.

"Damned if a half-smart lil part-*Pehnane* boy like me knows what to make of it," the Kid announced. "The gambler and the French gal've just come back from the corrals. Only she sure's not dressed for going riding any place 'cept bed."

"How do you mean?" Dusty asked.

"There's a couple of saddled hosses down where they come from," explained the Kid. "And, to put the lid on the whole boiling, he's gone to the barn and she's headed for the cookshack."

"What do you make of it, Dusty?" Breda inquired.

"I'm damned if I know," the small Texan replied. "Let's go and find out."

Continuing their advance, Libby and Dusty separated

from the remainder of the posse. Having a shorter distance than their companions to cover, they took up their position and studied their surroundings. Lights glowed in all three buildings which did not surprise them. Suddenly Libby gripped Dusty's left arm and pointed to where a man and woman had appeared from the side door of the house.

"It's the 'de Brioudes'!" Libby breathed. "She's sending him to the barn."

Crouching motionless, the blonde and Dusty watched the French couple. After her husband had walked off in the direction of the barn's front entrance, Béatrice turned and entered the house through the side door.

"Hell's fire!" Dusty spat out. "This changes everything. Go and get Tam, Libby, *pronto*!"

"Why?" the blonde asked.

"Stagge's waiting in the barn, fixing to kill that feller and burn him and Laura!" Dusty snapped and darted away before Libby could say another word.

Once again the small Texan had made an accurate guess at what his enemies planned to do. He based his findings on what the Kid had seen and the incident he had just witnessed. With the horses saddled and waiting, there could hardly be any other reason for Béatrice to send her husband into the barn. Only two mounts waited ready for use, while Stagge and the injured Laura were in the barn.

Shocked by the sheer callous nature of the scheme, Dusty held himself in control and refused to be panicked into acting recklessly. To take the shortest route to the front of the barn meant going alongside the house. Dusty faced the same danger as his companions if he passed by the end of the main living quarters. If he did so, Béatrice might see or hear him. In which case, she would raise the alarm before the cookshack was surrounded. Let that happen and the hard-cases would burst out. All too well Dusty knew the perils of a number of men fighting in the darkness. As a result of the confusion, a friend could easily be shot instead of an enemy. Determined to avoid that if he could, Dusty ran along the rear of the barn. He hoped to be able to effect an entrance from there.

Watching her companion go, Libby let out an indignant sniff. While she did not doubt that Dusty had excellent reasons for leaving her, she felt disinclined to accept the part assigned to her. If she carried out her instructions, the Frenchwoman might still escape. Anyway, as Libby saw it, she was the one best fitted to deal with Béatrice whatever-her-real-name-might-be.

Setting her lips into grimly determined lines, Libby went to the side door. She had visited the house when the Renfrews owned it and knew that the door led into the main room. Carefully operating the handle, she eased the main door. Its hinges creaked a little, but there was no immediate challenge to her entry. A lamp glowed from the center of the ceiling and the robe Béatrice had been wearing lay on the floor.

"Who is that?" demanded the Frenchwoman from the nearer bedroom.

Moving fast, but silently, Libby went to and flattened herself against the wall at the right of the door. She only just reached her position in time.

"Arnaud!" Béatrice called, in French. "Have you done it already?"

While speaking, the "Vicomtesse" walked out of the bedroom. She was buttoning a blouse, but still had not donned a skirt or sturdier footwear than her slippers. In passing, Béatrice caught a glimpse of Libby from a corner of her eye. However, the realization of what the sight meant came a moment too late. Stepping behind Béatrice, Libby hooked her left arm about the woman's throat. While doing so the blonde also tried to catch hold of the "Vicomtesse's" right wrist with her other hand. Although she failed to do so, Libby was not unduly concerned—at first.

Born in the Paris slums, Béatrice had learned early how to defend herself. On feeling Libby's arm about her throat, she reacted like a flash. While her two hands flew up to take a hold of the blonde's hair, she dropped her left knee to the floor. Sinking down and bending forward, she dragged her attacker off balance. Libby's feet left the floor. Passing over Béatrice's shoulders, she landed rump-first on the hard wooden planks.

The force of her efforts threw Béatrice forward along Libby's body. Almost by instinct, the blonde raised and wrapped her thighs about the "Vicomtesse's" head. Any relief Béatrice might have experienced at escaping from the first attack ended as Libby's ankles crossed and she began to apply the pressure with a vicelike power. Desperately Béatrice thrashed her legs and body around, while her fingernails raked ineffectually at Libby's Levi's-protected thighs.

Gritting her teeth and flailing punches at Béatrice's body, Libby thought she sensed her leg-hold slipping. The "Vicomtesse" felt a slight lessening of the constriction as the blonde sought to improve her grip. Taking her chance, Béatrice twisted her head and sank her teeth hard into Libby's inner thigh. Although the fingernails had had no effect against the Levi's material, Libby shrieked when the pain of the bite struck home. Again Béatrice clamped down her teeth, bringing a second cry from the blonde and the scissor-grip sprang open.

Croaking in relief, the Frenchwoman rolled across the floor. She wanted to be clear of any repetition of the agonizing hold. Hands flashing to her throbbing left thigh, Libby forced herself into a sitting position. They made it to their feet almost at the same moment.

"All right!" Libby gritted, still rubbing at her thigh. "I'm taking you—"

"Daughter of a whore!" Béatrice screeched back, but in French.

All the "Vicomtesse's" pent-up hatred for Libby boiled over. While speaking, she flung herself forward with hands reaching to claw or clutch flesh. That proved the wrong kind of tactics against Libby. Always something of a tomboy, the blonde had lived a life in which she had to be self-reliant. So her husband had improved upon her childhood lessons in self-defense. Trader had always told her that using clenched fists was a more effective protection than hair-yanking. Backing his words with instructions, he had left her well prepared for such an eventuality.

Bouncing forward, Libby swerved her head and torso clear of Béatrice's hands. Avoiding them, she hooked her right fist into the "Vicomtesse's" belly. The blow halted Béatrice's charge. Driven back a pace, the Frenchwoman caught her balance and hurled a wild right. Wild or not, it took Libby in the left breast an instant before her right drove into Béatrice's mouth.

Fists flew and the women came together, each trying to get inside the other's punishing blows. Suddenly Béatrice changed her tactics. Throwing her right arm across Libby's left shoulder, she jerked the blonde forward. Up swung Béatrice's right knee, colliding with Libby's belly. Clutching at the stricken area, the blonde let out a croaking cry and nausea threatened to overcome her.

Allowing her assailant to stumble away, gagging and crouching almost double, Béatrice turned and dived into the bedroom. Sobbing for breath, Libby staggered and almost fell. Sheer guts alone kept her on her feet. Battling down an inclination to collapse in an effort to lessen the torment, she started at the door through which her enemy had disappeared. Nor did Libby have long to wait before she learned why Béatrice had not followed up her advantage. Face distorted with rage, blood dribbling from her nostrils to splash on to the bosom bared by her ripped-open blouse, the "Vicomtesse" appeared again. Blade extending below it, her right hand gripped a knife. Mouthing French obscenities, Béatrice rushed across the room. Up swung the knife, ready to drive its spear-point down into the near-helpless Libby.

Having adorned Laura's drugged, unresisting body with Béatrice's jewelry, Stagge dragged her into a straw-filled stall. Leaving her as if she was no more than a piece of dead meat, the killer gave thought to his other preparations. From the look of the barn, it would blaze as if made of the so-called "Greek fire" incendiary compound use by both sides during the War. Once set alight, little would remain of the building.

An old pick handle lay by one wall. Picking it up, Stagge hefted it and decided that he had found the ideal weapon for dealing with "de Brioude." Better by far than trying to pistol-whip the man with his Colt Wells Fargo revolver. While the short-barreled gun served his purposes better than would a heavier weapon most of the time, it made a poor club. Pick handle in his right hand, he went to the front entrance. On coming in, he had opened only the left side of the twin doors. Concealing himself behind the right door, he strained his ears to catch the sound of "de Brioude's" approach.

When the footsteps became audible, Stagge gripped the upper end of the handle in both hands. One blow from that stout piece of timber would be enough to render the "Vicomte" unconscious, if not dead, and the fire would do the rest. People would assume that a falling beam or something had struck him down when they found his body. By that time, Stagge would be on his way to the border and, as long as she behaved herself, accompanied by the "Vicomtesse."

Nearer came the footsteps. Stagge tensed, crouching and holding the handle like a batsman awaiting the pitcher's delivery of the ball. In the light of the solitary lantern left burning to illuminate the interior, the killer could see well enough for his purposes. Two, three at most, more steps would bring "de Brioude" through the door.

Then the "Vicomte" entered. Looking neither right nor left, he increased his pace slightly. Silently Stagge stepped into position. He swung the handle with all his strength, aiming it at the back of "de Brioude's" skull—and missed.

Almost as if expecting the attack, "de Brioude" suddenly bent his knees and ducked beneath the whistling arc of the missile. Displaying an equal agility, he bounded backward. On landing, he pivoted on one foot and lashed a kick in Stagge's direction with the other. Luck saved the killer from taking the impact on his groin. His uninterrupted impetus caused him to spin around. Instead of "de Brioude's" foot reaching his testicles, it caught him on the hip.

Yelping in pain, Stagge stumbled and dropped the pick handle. Twisting his head, he saw for the first time that "de Brioude's" left hand gripped a heavy double-barreled pistol. Fury blasted through Stagge as the implications of the discovery hit him. For "de Brioude" to have arrived armed, taking care to conceal the weapon, Béatrice must have warned him of the trap. In which case, Stagge was to have been the male body found in the burned-out barn and not her husband.

Darting toward Stagge, "de Brioude" swung around the pistol. The killer threw up his left arm to protect his head. Steel met bone with a vicious thud and Stagge's arm dropped limply to his side. Crying out in pain, he reeled hurriedly away from his assailant. At any moment, he expected the Frenchman's pistol to line and roar out its load at him. Instead, "de Brioude" advanced with his hand drawing back to hit again.

In a flash of inspiration, the killer realized why "de Brioude" did not shoot. To do so would bring the other men from the cookshack and ruin the scheme to make the French couple's enemies believe they had perished in the fire. Stagge need have no such concern. With "de Brioude" dead, Buck-Eye—Stagge still did not know of the lanky man's desertion—and the rest would willingly share his property. That could include the "Vicomtesse" for all the killer cared.

Across flashed Stagge's right hand, going under his jacket. Recognizing his peril, "de Brioude" staked all on a desperate leap. With the old pistol swinging wickedly toward his head, Stagge completed his draw and planted a .31 ball between the Frenchman's eyes. The blow collapsed in mid-delivery and "de Brioude" spun around. Even as he fell, there was a crash and the rear door flew open.

From delivering a *karate* kick that served as well as any key, Dusty plunged into the barn. He saw "de Brioude" going down in the rag doll-limp manner of a man shot in the head. Cocking the small revolver, Stagge turned it in Dusty's direction. Drawing his right side Colt as he finished his entrance in a rolling dive, Dusty aimed and fired as he landed. His aim proved just as accurate, and fatal, as Stagge's at the Frenchman. Hit in the head by Dusty's bullet, Stagge joined "de Brioude" on the floor of the barn.

At the cookshack, the Kid had just reached the front door when he heard the shooting at the barn. Forgetting about giving the signal, he ducked his shoulder and charged at the door. Crashing in, he lined his Winchester at waist level toward the men around the table. Windows shattered and other doors opened forcibly as the rest of the Kid's party displayed an equally shrewd judgment of the changed situation. With weapons lining from all sides, the occupants of the shack could do nothing but surrender. To have tried otherwise would have asked for certain death and they were just sober enough to know it.

"Disarm them, Félix, Mark," Tam Breda ordered. "Bernardo, go find out what the shooting's abou—"

The scream of a woman in mortal pain chopped off the peace officer's words.

CHAPTER SEVENTEEN

Never had Béatrice Argile been in such a complete, savage, uncontrollable rage as while she rushed, knife in hand, toward Libby Schell.

After outwitting the police in Europe's two most civilized countries—the Argiles had operated half of their time in England—and evading the efforts to trap them made by two powerful criminal organizations, they had been foiled and defeated at the hands of a bunch of half-primitive country bumpkins.

What was more, Béatrice could blame it all on that fat old woman who cowered in terror before her. If Libby Schell had not interfered in the affair of *le beau* Counter at Fort Sawyer, none of this would have happened. Béatrice and her husband would have continued with the hunting expedition until sure that they were not followed by their enemies, or until whoever came had been killed by Stagge, then settle down somewhere in the United States and live as the Vicomte and Vicomtesse de Brioude. Instead, goaded by hatred, Béatrice had insisted on following the blonde and Counter to Kerr County where she had seen and set her heart on owning the horse called Mogollon.

Although she did not realize it, assuming the identity of the Vicomtesse de Brioude had been Béatrice's worst mistake. The treatment she had been accorded since the transformation differed greatly from when she had posed as a maid. On the long boat journey and since arriving in the United States, people had done everything she asked and almost fallen over backward in their eagerness to please her. So Béatrice had grown accustomed to being allowed her own way and enjoyed it. Colin Farquharson's refusal to sell Mogollon had infuriated her, continuing the train of events which had led her to disaster and ruin.

The sound of shooting from the barn had reached Béatrice's ears without lessening her determination to kill Libby Schell. For all his habit of gambling at every opportunity, she had considered Arnaud a better prospect than Stagge. By pretending to agree to it, she had learned the killer's scheme for escaping. Then she had secretly modified it. Collecting her husband from the cookshack, she had brought him to the house. When he had heard what Stagge planned, Arnaud collected one of his—or the Vicomte de Brioude's— pistols and went to reverse the arrangements by making the killer the victim. The pistol had been unloaded and meant to be used as a club. Which implied that the firing had been done by Stagge—and another person.

Most likely the second shooter belonged to the Schell woman's party, for the blonde would never have come unescorted. Somehow they had arrived undetected by Buck-Eye, or he had deserted and fled on hearing them coming. Prison awaited Béatrice, of that she felt certain, and with it, reports of newspapers circulated in France. When she was released, her enemies would know where to find her. She might find them waiting for her on her release—but Libby Schell would not live to see it happen.

Swinging the knife high above her head, Béatrice started to deliver a downward, killing blow.

Libby Schell came from a sturdy, hardy fighting stock which did not give up without a struggle, no matter how great the odds. Filled with nausea, winded and a little dazed, she had watched Béatrice charging at her. Retaining her appearance of beaten incomprehension, she mustered up all her reserves of strength. Although she had to exert every grain of her will-power, she forced herself to remain inactive until the correct moment.

Placing her left hand on the right so that their thumbs formed a V, she flung them up. She trapped Béatrice's wrist from underneath and with the knife's blade pointing between her arms. Instead of trying to halt the thrust, Libby jerked downward. By drawing back her torso, she avoided the attack. Almost scraping the front of Libby's bosom in passing, the knife's spear point continued to descend until it spiked into the upper inside part of the "Vicomtesse's" right thigh. The combined impetus of Béatrice's blow and Libby's pull caused the blade to sink hilt-deep into her flesh, cutting the femoral artery in passing.

A hideous scream burst from the Frenchwoman. So horrible did it sound that Libby released her hold and staggered away. Trying to withdraw the knife, while blood spurted from the wound, Béatrice reeled. Then she dropped to her knees and sank forward, fainting through loss of blood and pain.

For once in her life, Libby came close to hysterics. Staggering to the side door by which she had entered, she heard the front entrance smashed open. Tam Breda rushed in, caught Libby in his arms and hustled her out of the room.

Half an hour later, having regained her composure, Libby sat in the cookshack and listened to her companions' stories. All the "de Brioudes'" hired men had been questioned, without adding much to what was already known, and released under orders to leave Kerr County by the shortest, quickest route. Sent for by Dusty—using a sullen but obedient Sergeant Heaps as the messenger—the Kerrville doctor had arrived and was at that moment ministering to Laura.

"And it's all over," Major Aarhorte commented. "There'll be a few important folk relieved about how it came out."

True to his promise, the major had brought up his men when the shooting started. Their services had not been needed, except to help with the cleaning up and removal of the bodies.

"Sure," Dusty agreed. "The 'de Brioudes' couldn't've been deported without the newspapers getting hold of the story. It would've embarrassed everybody who'd been taken in by them."

"Are you all right, Mrs. Schell?" Inspector Fontaine inquired, studying her bruised, still somewhat pallid face.

"I'll do," Libby assured him and gently touched her swollen, discolored left eye. "If a peace officer's wife has to go through things like this, I'm not sure I want to be one."

"There's your chance, Tam!" whooped the Ysabel Kid. "Get to running for the hills afore she changes her mind."

"If he tries, I'll break both his legs," Libby threatened. "And yours, you blasted *Pehnane*, for suggesting it."

Two weeks later, on the eve of what would be a double wedding, Tam Breda stood with his arm around Libby's waist and watched Jeanie mount Mogollon. Gathered along the corral's fence, Colin, the floating outfit and the *mesteneros* waited to see what happened. With a deft swing, the girl lowered herself astride the saddle. At first Mogollon snorted and fiddle-footed, but Jeanie had been around so much with Colin that it accepted her.

"Damned if it's right," growled the Kid, nudging Colin in the ribs.

"What?" asked the Scot.

"Seeing a she-male riding a man's war-hoss," the dark youngster explained. "Which ole Mogollon sure don't look too happy about it, neither. That's the worst of being catched and all tamed down, man or beast—"

"He's smart enough to know when he's well off," Colin declared, interrupting the Kid's views on how being "catched and all tamed down" affected man or beast. "No more roaming the range, being chased and harassed. He'll have a good home, female company and somebody to take care of him when he's old and worn out."

"Is that Mogollon you're talking about, *amigo*," Dusty inquired, "or you?"

"Both, I reckon," Colin admitted and watched with pride as his wife-to-be rode around the corral on the horse called Mogollon.

Raw, fast-action adventure from one of the world's favorite Western authors
MAX BRAND

0-425-10190-8	DAN BERRY'S DAUGHTER	$2.75
0-425-10346-3	RIDERS OF THE SILENCES	$2.75
0-425-10420-6	DEVIL HORSE	$2.75
0-425-10488-5	LOST WOLF	$2.75
0-425-10557-1	THE STRANGER	$2.75
0-425-10636-5	TENDERFOOT	$2.75
0-425-10761-2	OUTLAW BREED	$2.75
0-425-10869-4	TORTURE TRAIL	$2.75
0-425-10992-5	MIGHTY LOBO	$2.75
0-425-11027-3	THE LONG CHASE	$2.75
	(On sale June '88)	
0-425-11065-6	WAR PARTY (On sale July '88)	$2.75

writing as Evan Evans

0-515-08711-4	SIXGUN LEGACY	$2.75
0-515-08776-9	SMUGGLER'S TRAIL	$2.95
0-515-08759-9	OUTLAW VALLEY	$2.95
0-515-08885-4	THE SONG OF THE WHIP	$2.75

Please send the titles I've checked above. Mail orders to:

BERKLEY PUBLISHING GROUP
390 Murray Hill Pkwy., Dept. B
East Rutherford, NJ 07073

NAME_____

ADDRESS_____

CITY_____

STATE_____ZIP_____

Please allow 6 weeks for delivery.
Prices are subject to change without notice.

POSTAGE & HANDLING:
$1.00 for one book, $.25 for each additional. Do not exceed $3.50.

BOOK TOTAL	$_____
SHIPPING & HANDLING	$_____
APPLICABLE SALES TAX (CA, NJ, NY, PA)	$_____
TOTAL AMOUNT DUE	$_____

PAYABLE IN US FUNDS.
(No cash orders accepted.)

WANTED:
Hard Drivin' Westerns From

J.T.Edson

__ APACHE RAMPAGE	0-425-09714-5/$2.50
__ THE BAD BUNCH	0-425-09897-4/$2.75
__ THE COLT AND THE SABRE	0-425-09341-7/$2.50
__ HELL IN THE PALO DURO	0-425-09361-1/$2.50
__ THE HIDE AND TALLOW MEN	0-425-08744-1/$2.50
__ KILL DUSTY FOG!	0-441-44110-6/$2.75
__ THE QUEST FOR BOWIE'S BLADE	0-425-09113-9/$2.50
__ THE REBEL SPY	0-425-09646-7/$2.50
__ RETURN TO BACKSIGHT	0-425-09397-2/$2.50
__ SET TEXAS BACK ON HER FEET	0-425-08651-8/$2.50
__ THE TEXAS ASSASSIN	0-425-09348-4/$2.50
__ THE TRIGGER MASTER	0-425-09087-6/$2.50
__ UNDER THE STARS AND BARS	0-425-09782-X/$2.50
__ WACO'S DEBT	0-425-08528-7/$2.50
__ THE YSABEL KID	0-425-08393-4/$2.50
__ COMANCHE	1-55773-038-5/$2.75
__ CARDS AND COLTS	1-55773-029-6/$2.75

Please send the titles I've checked above. Mail orders to:

BERKLEY PUBLISHING GROUP
390 Murray Hill Pkwy., Dept. B
East Rutherford, NJ 07073

POSTAGE & HANDLING:
$1.00 for one book, $.25 for each
additional. Do not exceed $3.50.

NAME_____

ADDRESS_____

CITY_____

STATE_____ZIP_____

Please allow 6 weeks for delivery.
Prices are subject to change without notice.

BOOK TOTAL $_____

SHIPPING & HANDLING $_____

APPLICABLE SALES TAX $_____
(CA, NJ, NY, PA)

TOTAL AMOUNT DUE $_____
PAYABLE IN US FUNDS.
(No cash orders accepted.)